3ʳᵈ Hand Ranch

By L.R. Claude:

I can't thank enough; the life
changing events that transpire when you
become a parent and how the changes
amass into a more fulfilled person.

*Sometimes all you may have is yourself,
if you don't like who you are or have
become, you still have the dream of who
you can become.*

-L.R. Claude

3RD HAND RANCH

My name is Austin Monroe, I am in my mid thirties and married to a wonderful woman named Rebecca. Rebecca and I run a small sheep farm called the 3rd Hand Ranch, my ranch has five horses of ours plus one we board for a friend. Rebecca is a fulltime nurse while I am mainly a farmer and subcontract writing manuals for a research company sometimes. Rebecca and I met in college and both shared the dream of running a fully operational ranch. I usually have around fifty sheep, a dozen or so chickens and my best mate Banjo.

Banjo is a goofy Australian shepherd, he does a wonderful job herding the sheep and moving the flock from one grazing area to another. I took classes at Eastern Michigan University for freelance writing and established myself very early on. I was fortunate to gather many contracts when I began and shortly after college; my wife and I started the beginnings of our ranch. Rebecca loved horses, as many young girls do. We toiled to build everything we had during our young twenties. We married in June of 2000 and purchased a two-hundred acre plot of farm land that had been foreclosed on.

The home on the property was in rough shape, I wrote during the dark hours or while Beck was working, and together we gutted the house and rebuilt it almost from the ground up. To date we have a beautiful five bedroom home that we had hoped to fill with children. Banjo joined us as a tiny six week old a few years back as we bred sheep and grew our herd. I had some friends help me build our large barns and I have since built paddocks for horses to graze in also. The property is rather diverse to serve all the needs of the farm and the critters that are spread out all over.

A few years after we were married, Rebecca and I found out that we were unable to have children. We were devastated, we had diligently worked so very hard to build a home to produce offspring, we poured our hearts and selves into a home that we wanted to flourish within. We have a modest farm in comparison to the many others in the county but it serves a grand purpose and it has birthed directly from our dreams. About a year ago Rebecca had a new dream; we both dreamed of filling our home with children and other than banjo, our home was fairly silent these last several years. The silence was disheartening but it still teemed with our love.

Aussies are a smart breed and Banjo was always into something, we looked at him like a three year old and he was always playful. Banjo sat outside the chicken pen and would rub against it checking for weaknesses. Banjo didn't ever want to hurt any of the birds but chasing them seemed to be his desire every time. Banjo took to herding quickly, with minimal training, it was instinctive and his real job around the ranch. Banjo was a tri-color merle, he was mostly white, had splotches of black and light brown speckled all over him and the spots on his face gave him character in his facial expressions.

Rebecca's newest dream was to possibly adopt, the process was long and drawn out. It was sad that there were so many kids in need of loving homes but the paperwork and red-tape made it next to impossible to adopt kids from our own country. I had about twenty acres for the paddocks, a one-hundred acre plot for growing hay and two thirty acre chunks for sheep grazing, another ten acres that the house, barn and other outbuildings sat upon. Rebecca and I enjoyed gardening during the warm Michigan summers, we froze and canned most of what we grew, I had ample supplies to sell to a good friend Sampson that ran a small market a few miles away.

Sampson had a small butchery attached to his market and I would sell many sheep to him for sale or trading of supplies. Sampson also sold a lot of my hay in exchange for most of the horse feed that I needed year round. Sampson Douglas was an older gentleman, his wife Eugenia passed away a few years back from diabetic complications but he still took great pride in his son Freddie and daughter in-law Gloria. Freddie was a corporal in the Air force and was stationed in Texas but it was good seeing Freddie when he made the trip back north. Sampson was a well-liked man in the area and to his credit; was almost to cool for his own good.

Rebecca's dream of adopting grew dark and each time we submitted paperwork or jumped through another hoop, it seemed the dream got farther from grasp each time. Rebecca had a younger sister Kaylee that was six years younger than she was and an intelligent young lady. Kaylee passed away a few years back as a victim of very bleak circumstances. Kaylees death left my wife an only child and that further propagated her desire to start a family. Having to bury the young twenty-three year old pre-law student was a trying time for us, I held her tight every night for a year and she still weeps from time to time.

Many of my days start out shoveling and cleaning stalls, moving horses and running drills with Banjo to keep the sheep from eating holes in one place or another. During the spring and summer I get three hay cuttings from the fields and have to stack and pile the bales. The day after the cuttings I let the sheep wander the cut fields to eat at the dead hay and fertilize the grounds for two days. I have the fields cut unevenly so the sheep can eat plenty and fertilize the grounds. I also spread the waste piles from the horses over the fields and get good hay from each cutting.

Most of my days are fairly busy and they go faster when I have the help of my wife by my side.

On *her* days off we manage our chores much faster and we spend free nights having cookouts with friends from the small town. Banjo loves Sampson because Sampson will often "drop" a scrap or two and as quickly as he swoops around sheep and ducks back down, Banjo quickly snipes a piece of food and ducks off to hide and eat. I'm not sure who I yell at more, Sampson or Banjo when they get together. They are great pals and Sampsons' big loving heart exudes at everything he does.

Each spring the lambs arrive, on good years we'll get better than twenty little baby lambs showing up in the pasture and it's a nice surprise each time. Rebecca will give shots to the babies and I'll recruit the help of my pal Mike to help hold and sheer the thick coats when he has a free weekend. Mike is a principal at the high school and he and his brother Randy get down and dirty with me in the country when I need the help. Mike is married to Annie, whom is great friends with my wife. The wives sit and sip lemonade or other assorted drinks and complain about the heat while we men bust our backs in the hot days' sun.

Last spring Rebecca came across a heart wrenching story of a young girl bullied to death by a group of juvenile delinquents that found it funny. It was a tragedy for such a situation to occur and it was almost too gruesome to comprehend as reality. Rebecca took on nursing because she had a large heart and was infinitely caring. The suicide reawakened her emotions that she had struggled with after the tragic passing of her sister. After the news story; Rebecca was stricken sick with guilt and her desire to help almost overtook her.

Rebecca hatched a plan that was fairly detailed and involved but it was doable and it consumed her. Rebecca wished with her whole being that she could have helped; the young girl that took her own life had to have been tormented to such a degree that no one could comprehend in order to push her to suicide. The young girl that had killed herself was a beautiful young lady, much like Kaylee was and for the world to let an innocent youth and endless center of talent, leave this world, was beyond tragic.

Rebecca propositioned me that she wanted to help; she wanted to prevent such a situation that would ever force someone down the road that led to the taking of their own life. The realistic aspects of trying to help thousands of lost young girls was of such a magnitude that it surpassed impossibility. Rebecca shaved off the delusions of grandeur and her revision was much more realistic. Rebecca wanted to try to either adopt or just talk to some of the girls that needed the desperate help that she felt she could offer. The issues that followed last spring were still pretty large, how would she get to them or what could she do?

During the spring she was so focused on her new mission that I often had to regain her attention when we were performing our chores. I loved seeing my wife with hope in her heart but I felt bad that she was so consumed with grief over the tragedies of life that it upset her stomach and sometimes overwhelmed her. I felt terrible that my wife felt so helpless in many ways. Beck took great pride in her job as a nurse and it gave her the ability to help many people day in and day out. I wondered how she could keep helping when many of her patients passed on but she was at peace with the knowledge that she was able to help, even if only a little.

The spring brought us many baby lambs to handle and the purchase of a new horse. The newest horse was a big black stallion, he was officially named "Ace of Spades" and he was a thoroughbred race horse, recently retired, I renamed him Lemmy because he was a grungy handful and a bit of a stubborn jerk. Lemmy became our fifth horse but sixth in all that we had in our barn. I boarded a horse named Elvis for another friend of Rebecca's, Elvis was owned by the high-school counselor named Felicia Kieme. Felicia fell in love with Elvis and just had to have him but lived in the city with no ability to board him, one quick phone call and a heavy "*pleeeease*" to my wife and I got another horse to care for.

My first horse was a white mare with gray speckles all over named Harpo. Harpo was a farm pony and she was a silly heart. Harpo was very trustable, you could let go of her lead rope in an open field and she would just follow you around, except if you reached for the lead, she would whip her head back so you missed it each time. Harpo was acquired because Beck wanted a horse to ride around the property and even though I have a truck to do most of my work, it was helpful at times to have her haul logs from the woods when I was stockpiling lumber for firewood.

A year after I bought Harpo I bought two more horses, a brown horse with black mane I named Groucho and a caramel colored one I named Chico. The summer after Grouch and Chico arrived, Rebecca brought home a painted mare she named Zeppo. I loved having the Marx Brothers themed horses but in reality, I had no real need for more than one. The horses were fun but they served very little purpose having them around the farm for any more than proving it was a farm. I stocked two-thirds of the hay I cut and sold a few hundred bales through Sampson's' market.

Sampson's market was a well-rounded mini-mart with a deli counter, many shelves of groceries and also a back wall pin board full of flyers for farm supplies or growers, and this was how I sold most of my hay. Each morning I would lead the horses out to paddocks for grazing and begin to shovel stalls. I would cart out the waste to a big compost pile that I would turn weekly until it was time to spread on the fresh cut hay fields for fertilizer. The front of the barn served as the garage, above the garage was for hay bale storage and the back of the barn was for the horse stalls. The barn is a basic metal building but it served a great purpose in all that I did.

The sheep had a barn that saddled two pastures and all I had to do was decide which door to open to let most of them out. I had a staging pen so we could mark the babies and hold the adults for shearing, sheep were a fair amount of work but in all honesty, they were pretty low maintenance. It was easy with Banjo at my side when it came to working the flock, a working sheep dog was worth a few people when they were trained well. Banjo kept me on my toes plenty but he was a good boy and an even better friend. Banjo was up before the sun with me and he ran all day long, on days when he wasn't being worked he was extra rambunctious and he would play fetch, or tug for hours, or end up in mischief.

I had a three part chicken pen and only housed a dozen or two birds. I kept a hen pen for egg layers, a breeding pen which housed four females and an arrogant rooster and also a smaller pen that had the chicks until they were big enough to defend themselves. The chickens hardly needed much more than feed and water daily, Banjo would get rough and want to lick the chicks after they hatched before we put them in the little pen, I had no idea what Banjos' deal was but he had something for those bloody chickens. When I had enough extra chickens or an overabundance of eggs I would drop off the extra to Sampson and he would keep track of what the balances were.

My business with Sampson was evenly distributed
and a fair quid pro quo. I would usually exchange
many of my goods for groceries from his store and
anytime he would call me up it was usually to
request a lamb or two for his meat counter. There
was a small butcher shop out behind his store and
he made sure the animals were put down as fast
and painless as possible, he had a main butcher
named Winston. Winston was also a colored guy,
much younger than Sampson but also of high
caliber. Winston grew up in a small town and came
to live with an uncle to keep out of trouble.
Winston had a good head on his shoulders, was well
educated and very well spoken.

Winston went to school in Ypsilanti and with
friends like that; jail usually isn't too far behind.
Winston foresaw his path if he had continued
following his friends and he quickly made a smart
choice to bail on the risk of ending up dead. I
admired Winston for his good choice; he was a
hard worker and saved everything he made for
college in the next year or so. Sampson took to
Winston like a replacement for Freddie and they
got along very well.

As spring ramped up I had no idea what the
following year would entail as it unfolded but I had
my wife by my side, my best mate Banjo to keep me
company and a plethora of friends to rely on if
anything were to come up. Rebecca came up with a
plan of action and she sprung it on me one early
Saturday morning as we led horses into their

respective pastures. Rebecca explained that she wanted to seek out some of the young girls that were in such a bad place and that without help, they were destined to commit suicide. I asked her how she planned to find these young women and what she was going to do from there.

Apparently my wife, Beck, had been talking with her friends Felicia and Annie and all of them felt just as sick over the situations that caused some of the girls to show up on news sites having killed themselves. It was becoming an epidemic and something had to be done. I couldn't blame the ladies for feeling like something had to be done, especially my wife, but I was still at a loss to what could really be done. Beck told me about her plans and how they pieced together as she dreamed. She also explained that she didn't want to feel horrible anymore about not trying something. Becks' plan of action was to try to locate a few girls that were at their worst and contact them.

I questioned her plans for once the girls were located and had to convince her to "land the plane" meaning to spit out the meat of the topic and quit fiddling with the potatoes of the matter. Finally after Lemmy was secured in his holding paddock and she was done beating around the bush, she stared quietly at me for a moment before her mouth opened.

My wife had short light brown hair she kept dusted with highlights, her green eyes made my knees weak each time she looked deeply into mine. I felt that each time my wife looked into my eyes that she could see all the bad things I have ever done and forgive each one. I was at ease with her in my life and I was most fortunate that she chose me to make me her life partner. We worked very well together and deeply respected open honesty and knew that it was a grave key to a fruitful relationship. Rebecca and I hardly fought but would playfully toy at each other's nerves once in a while and we would accuse each other of buying Banjos' loyalty depending on the topic of disagreement.

Beck finally took a deep barn dust filled breath before starting to unfurl her idea. I knew from her choppy sleep over the last few nights that she was up to something but I also knew that it was pointless to dig at her about it until she had it worked out for herself. Rebecca pondered for a moment about her wording but I already knew that she had rehearsed it a multitude of times before confronting me. Rebecca suggested that we should locate several girls that need the help and offer it, I tossed her a mildly blank look, heavily strewn with "DUHHH" but I suspected her hesitation in delivering the final main idea was for lack of confidence.

Beck wanted to fly out or drive to meet with the girls that she or her friends were able to track down from the internet and meet with the parents. She wanted to convince the girls to come join us at the ranch for a school year and give them a school year free of the social media plague or devoid of the bullying that may have pushed them to such grim mental imprisonment. I couldn't respond to her idea immediately and to be honest it kinda made my head spin a bit and I needed time to think it over.

I acknowledged that I understood what she was saying and I knew that her heart was very set on helping. I was overwhelmed with all of the information and there was so much to process to get to point Z from point A before even making any progress to the next step if this were to take form. My head began to spin and I got to shoveling stalls as Beck went out to brush horses and we got to our chores to finish up our morning. Banjo scurried about between Beck and I trying to keep the majority of our attention and distract us from our task at hand. I had so much to process as I thought about all the angles of what would happen if we suddenly started importing girls to our farm.

I worried about all the liabilities and risks of girls with no farm hand experience and what if Lemmy kicked one of them in one of his piss head fits or even worse; what if one of the girls accused me of something while Rebecca was at work because I was male? I tried to keep my focus on mixing feed buckets and cleaning up the barns, sweeping the rubber mats and dusting the areas that filled with cobwebs. I peeked out the door occasionally to keep an eye on my wife, I loved having her with me at home and she was always playing with Banjo without me. Banjo was a great friend and his loving manner was so pleasant to have around the house.

The stalls didn't take all that long to shovel out but there was always the additional stuff, checking for holes that the horses sometimes created as they stomped at the ground, throwing fresh hay down on the floor and sweeping it all up. I mixed feed buckets and hung each one on the inner door of each stall for the horses when they returned. I hung new water buckets and made sure all the twine was tied up on the gate, if a horse happens to eat the twine then that's just about a death sentence for the horse as it would bind up in their intestines creating severe fatal pain and agony.

I had to sweep the infrared ceiling heaters every day, the cobwebs were thick and trapped a lot of the hay dust and would build up in the grates and pose a fire risk in the barn. Having several hundred bales of hay above the garage portion of the barn would make for a quick and violent fuel if a fire were to ignite. I was very vigilant about fire risks and even made sure the outlet covers had outdoor covers over them so dirt and grit wouldn't build up inside the outlets themselves, I had ceiling mounted infrared heaters all over for when it was really cold and I even had one in the garage for the old Ford truck I was trying to rebuild.

I was only able to wrench a few hours here and there on the old truck; I was traded the body and parts for a hundred hale bales and a lamb by an old farmer named Robert Marion that needed the hay on the quick for some of his cows, he was strapped for the cash so I made the trade and hauled a wagon full of hay for him. I enjoyed the garage time while Banjo usually had a bone or something to toss around for himself. I was usually out there on the nights Rebecca picked up a night shift or stayed late so I was able to pass the time. Banjo loved throwing tennis balls so they bounced all over the garage and then he would run and chase them, I'd just talk to him as I worked.

Banjo was pretty good at keeping himself occupied and he behaved well even when he was bored. I would turn on an oldies station in the garage and keep my cell nearby. The cell service was shotty in the area so I ordered a booster that I had in the barn that gave me good service anywhere on the farm just in case something happened. The garage was the front of the barn and had two doors on the front but there was room for four cars, it housed my regular truck, Rebecca's car and buckshot, buckshot was the sixties truck I was hoping to restore.

The back of the barn behind the horse stalls is where I kept the four-wheeler I used around the farm. Along with various farm equipment; such as the manure spreader or the loading belt that I used to send hay bales up to the second story barn door above the garage doors. I loved that I was running a working farm and that I had a beautiful wife to do so by my side. We both took great pride in the detailed care we were able to provide for our animals and the produce that helped to serve fellow farmers in the area. Sampson's was a good central hub for many of the necessities that my farm needed most of the time.

Banjo would often need a brushing and it was a pleasant thing to do in the sunsets to end a day, or two a week. Banjo belly crawled around the chicken pens, he was rather goofy and as I mentioned, always wanted to play with the birds. Anytime a chicken gets out as I have to enter the pen and any time one of the feathered critters can manage past me, Banjo is usually right there to chase it about, he paced back and forth as it flapped its wings trying to out run him. Banjo never bit any of the birds; he just wanted to sniff the babies.

Rebecca had the grand idea of inviting a few girls to spend a school year as working guests at our farm. Mike was the principal at the high school so making the transition would be seamless and Becks' friend Felicia was the school counselor so there was a therapist that would be at our farm every Sunday when she came out to ride Elvis. There were riding trails around the property and through some of the surrounding woods, during the fall it was really peaceful. Beck and I often took out Harpo and another horse on runs to keep them used to being saddled.

Harpo was a goofy horse, her personality was screwy, her favorite thing to do was wait until your back is turned then she'll put her mouth right behind an ear and blow through her lips causing you to jump. I'm fairly used to it but she'll still startle me once in a while. Banjo was always by my side when I worked alone in the barn when Beck worked.

Banjo would always leave me to be a big boy when Beck was with me; he always knew that she would pet him much more than work when we were keeping to our chores.

Spring brought many new lambs; I had my hands full tagging the additions to the livestock. I would often crate a handful of birds and head to Sampson's so he had farm raised chickens to butcher and sell in his meat case. Winston was the main butcher and even though it was a bloody job, he seemed to stay remarkably clean. Mikes younger brother Randy was a skillful farmhand and he was usually the go to guy when I had hay to cut and stack hay. Rebecca and I discussed the many angles that might occur having four strangers staying with us, young girls that had absolutely zero farm knowledge.

I was unsure about how the turnout would end up. I questioned the end results and worried how attached Beck would get if we got a few girls to join us at the ranch and then return home after the school year. Would my caring wife be able to let go and move on? What if one of the girls followed through and ended their life at home after or even at our home? I had a multitude of concerns and taking on some teenage girls and whatever issues they may have. There is a lot to deal with when it came to teenagers, emotions and complications that I wasn't sure I could handle. I had confidence in my farm and how it ran but suddenly raising teens, was a significant shift of all sorts

I supported my wife and her idea was of sound intent, the issues that arose I worked through while I was working in the barns. I occasionally took on side writing jobs still here and there and the supplemental income always came in handy. Over the next couple weeks Beck and I discussed all of the complications we could figure and one Saturday night when the weather warmed up enough she and I had us a grilling party.

Mike and Annie joined us for some grilled chicken and drinks as Banjo played out as the prime entertainment. We group discussed the problems that might arise and what would be required to enroll a few girls into the high school as students and would have to include Felicia in our plans of action. Rebecca and I figured that we would try to convince a couple of girls to come join us at our home and learn a new way of life. Mike and Annie were on board and would help facilitate any necessary paperwork or take care of things in regards to the enrollment process.

We finished that night like so many before, the ladies' just giggling and playing with Banjo while Mike and I jawed about the farm and the upcoming summer and cutting seasons. The farm wasn't quiet by any means with the chickens, horses, sheep, and of course Banjo, and whatever he might be into but it was still very peaceful. I loved the sunsets on my farm and to take stock of how it all has come together under the fruitful work of Rebecca and I.

The Sunday morning following our barbecue, Felicia came out to work with Elvis. Felicia usually spent most of the day with her horse, she would spent ample time brushing him before saddling up and heading out to ride trails and circle the property. While Felicia was out riding she would eye the fences for me and check for any areas that the sheep might escape through or trees that might have fallen on the trails that went through the woods that we often walked with Banjo or rode horses through.

I didn't get to trail ride with my wife all that often but we tried once or twice a month, just for the sake of changing things up for us. More often than not, Rebecca and Felicia would ride together and be all girly and giggly the whole time, I didn't mind forfeiting riding time with them. Banjo and I always had plenty to keep us busy but sometimes he would leave me behind and go catch up with the ladies. Felicia was the school counselor and she was always busy in what she did, after school she would often coach the girls volleyball team and she was a good one.

As April came to a close, Beck was ramping up on her decision to move forward and she and her gaggle of ladies got to work keeping their eyes open for anyone in dire straits. Beck often picked up extra shifts and I would take on any writing assignment I could come across. Most of the work I picked up on were manuals for machines or new computer software for businesses. Most work I took on would run me better than a few weeks worth of research and work to do so I had plenty to keep me occupied.

Sheep can be stubborn critters, I had one big ram and I called him "Thickhead" and some days I wanted to load up that mean bugger and drop his shaggy hide off to Sampson and be done with him. Thickhead would stand his ground and often ram you right in the mid-thigh and oh it hurts. Thickhead would often chase Banjo and they seemed to be mortal enemies in the pastures. Banjo could herd the sheep and only when you moved most of his ladies' would Thickhead finally move to where he was supposed to. I often called Thickhead worse names and each time Beck caught me, she'd scold me and convince me that they all need to be spoken to in a nicer, loving manner.

Thickhead and Lemmy both gave me a fair amount of trouble between the two of them, neither understands that I am the man of the farm and some days I would love to punch them both in the head. Beck loved to sit back and watch Thickhead buck and ram me and he and I would just fight and struggle. Banjo didn't help enough when it came to Thickhead, I expected Banjo to keep that rowdy jerk off of me and keep him from whoopin' on me when I had to get into a pen or pasture and half the time; I was getting bucked before I realized Thickhead was on me. Man alive the charlie horses that Thickhead would leave from a quick buck from his horns to the thigh were just painful.

The farm ran pretty smoothly and to be honest, I wasn't sure how much things would change or how many challenges were ahead of me or us if we were to acquire some guests. On a Monday when Rebecca was at work, I went and met up with Mike and sought his opinion to Rebeccas' ideas and I needed his thoughts without the women around. I wasn't trying to undermine my wife but I was lacking experience in dealing with teenage girls and as a high school principal; Mike had many of the answers I needed, even if only for research information. Mike and I traded "what-if's" and the "what-nots" of things that might arise if this idea was to take shape. I really had a lot of real concerns, I wasn't saying Beck didn't worry but I think she was more focused on helping and may have been mildly blinded by the desire to help for her big heart to be fully realistic.

The last two weeks of April brought plenty of new lambs and spring cleaning around the farm. I often hired on Mike's younger brother Randy to help around the farm from time to time. Randy was always there when it came to cutting and bundling hay, he was a hard worker but always could manage to have a good time doing whatever he was doing. Randy worked hard and could throw a few hundred bales and still sit and crack a cold one while goofing around in the barn after a hard days work. I admired Randy's work ethic most of the time but sometimes you had to realign his focus on the task at hand when he got to chasing snakes or something in the hayfield.

Randy often had several jobs going for him at the same time but always dropped what he had going on to come throw some hay or get dirty at my farm, his help was always appreciated and I could rely on him. Randy and Mike often tussled when left to their own devices, of course being brothers it came naturally. Being a younger brother, Randy was usually the instigator and I usually spent half of a hay stacking day managing the brothers. I usually had Mike man the tractor while Randy and I bailed and stacked the hay. Randy was well familiar with many aspects of farming, he was a handy-man and could work all sorts of different machines and tools.

Randy was a giant contributor to a lot of the progress I've made around the farm. He had helped me dig and place the posts for the paddocks, build the barns as well as hang stalls and usually is by my side when it came to sheep shearing in the spring. Randy was dependable and a sturdy built guy, he was definitely an asset around the farm. Some nights when Rebecca worked late; Randy would stop by and just shoot the breeze with me in the barn after he spent the day wrenching or doing whatever he had on his to-do list that day.

One of the fun things was to grill out and have Randy and Mike on hand, between the two of them there was always someone being goofed on. Randy and Sampson often tried to outdo one another when it came to spoiling Banjo well beyond what he needed. Randy was usually the guy who Mike turned to when his school needed repair work during the summer and Mike made sure his younger brother was looked out for. I tried to return the favors to Randy when he needed a spare set of hands holding transmissions or hanging drywall.

I spent a Wednesday in mid-April with Beck working around the farm, We had plenty to do when it came to the sheep as well as giving all of them the spring shots and tags for the new ones. Beck and I spoke about her dream and how we were going to make this come to fruition. I explained my concerns and together, we worked out many of the finer details. Like everything else that we faced, we worked out everything; together. I loved my partner in life and her beauty was radiant and her heart was bigger than she was.

Rebecca and I spent our own time brushing our horses and giving them each our attention. I was often nervous with Lemmy as he was hard headed and stubborn as all get out. I often soothed the beast with sugar cubes and carrots, I was convinced this angry jerk was just not loved enough in his previous life as a racer and I was still hopeful that in time, he'd settle down and take to his new position as a farm horse. Lemmy was always kicking the stall walls and also at Banjo. Banjo steered clear of Lemmy and when Lemmy was out, Banjo was running and hiding from the massive horse.

I usually rubbed Lemmy's nose from the other side of the stall door and avoided his mouth as he always tried to bite me. Rebecca didn't work with Lemmy on her own but would grab a brush and work with him while I had him out. Lemmy eased a bit when we both brushed him but you could tell he tensed up when Banjo peaked around. Something about Banjo really made Lemmy nervous and we often had to lock Banjo in the screened in porch when we moved Lemmy around.

The summers were relaxing when the days came to an end and Rebecca and I were able to sit out and pet Banjo and just take stock of everything we had accomplished. We had a large farm and it has originated from an even larger dream. I was really impressed at the life that I had built with my wife. The work was hard some days but the end results of it were more than words could describe.

May came and Felicia was out to work with Elvis for her usual Sunday stroll. The weather never deterred her and she stuck by her word when it came to working with her horse every Sunday. Elvis was always glad to see her and every time her jeep pulled in, he would just get antsy and ready for his trail run, Felicia was semi-familiar with horses and she did pretty well at taking care of Elvis either brushing or saddling before spending an afternoon riding him.

That first Sunday in May Felicia had some tick on her mind when she came out to ride. Rebecca picked out Harpo to ride, the white horse was a very trustworthy horse and she was very gentle to ride. I was at ease whenever Rebecca rode Harpo or Chico as neither would ever buck her, I didn't suspect Groucho would either but I wasn't as certain because he was still one of the newer horses in the lot.

I was recruited to join the ladies in their afternoon ride and I took Groucho out that day. I'm sure Zeppo wanted to go out but I left him behind that time, I definitely wasn't going to take out Lemmy for the ride, I didn't trust that boy. As we rode our horses through the wooded trails and just walked and enjoyed the changing seasons, Felicia and Rebecca spoke and caught up while I surveyed the woods and property from the outer perimeter. I looked for weaknesses in the fences as well as what trees I was planning on cutting down for firewood.

Henry Ford once said "If you cut your own firewood, it'll warm you twice" I usually cut wood in the spring and let it dry all summer and then split it in the cooler fall days to feed into the fireplace in the living room or garage. I enjoyed chopping firewood, it's the best exercise you can get. Rebecca would often lay out in the nicer weather in the fall and just watch me chop wood, it was a good time for her and I won't lie, it was a romantic gesture I could perform for her.

I would often chainsaw a tree down and limb it then have Harpo and Chico drag it back while I rode Groucho. I could easily use a cart and the four-wheeler but it was fun going old school and using pure horsepower. The horses seemed to enjoy getting out and being able to graze on the longer wild grass or just to kick at the softer forest dirt. Of course, it didn't matter what I did, Banjo was always at my side or swooping back and forth behind us. It felt pretty rustic using horses to drag the wood but it was pretty fun.

Banjo was always a fan of me chopping wood, whenever a chunk would splinter off, he was quick to retrieve the wayward piece and chew it up until the next piece was available. It was actually kind of helpful because he would end up piling up the wood pieces and it was easier for me to clean up the mess when I was done chopping. Banjo wasn't intentionally cleaning up for me but he always chewed the pieces in the same spot so I ended up with one small pile instead of having to rake the mess up. My furry four-legged friend was a great help around the farm and he was a loved little sport.

Back to the conversation between Felicia and Rebecca, Felicia had a student discuss an internet video that was posted online and it was of a young girl asking for help. The video was silent but a young girl was holding up pieces of paper saying that she was in a bind, alone and desperate for a change or else she would have no choice but to kill herself. Felicia was at a loss that bullying left girls in such a situation that a blanket plea to the world was her only option.

Of course right away Rebecca wanted to do something; anything. After our ride we all sat and discussed what could be done as I fired up the grill and chatted into the late hours of the night. Felicia spoke about having had tracked down the video and how she spent most of the previous Friday on her task. Felicia was able to find the video and from that point she emailed the girls' account thing associated with the posting and told the girl that life was wonderful and nothing was worth throwing it away.

Felicia had pleaded to Rebecca and I to take on the task of locating this girl and trying to help. Rebecca and I weren't able to snap our fingers and just make things happen but we both felt that something had to be done. After Felicia left for the night; Rebecca and I spoke back and forth and tried to come up with a plan of action about how we would handle things if we could even reach this young girl and try to help.

Rebecca and I were at a loss for what we could do immediately and there was a small pain within us that nothing could be done instantly. I could tell by her restless sleep that night at the turmoil that kept her from peaceful sleep that she was sincerely troubled at the situation of this young girl. I loved my wife and her endearing heart to better this troubled world. I avoided the news as best I could because it was wrought with evil and ugliness. The news is depressing, it was disheartening that people were such selfish beings and the lack of community was a plague.

I was fortunate that I had such a loving lady by my side in this world and she had my whole heart. Come Monday I took to my chores and got everything done for the horses, I was playing catch with Banjo when my phone rang, Beck hardly ever called me from work as she was usually busy and I was tasked with ample chores to fill my days. Beck called to tell me that Felicia had called her at work and had received a response email from the young lady from the internet video. Felicia said the young ladies name was Harley Navarre and that she was 15 years old.

Harley Navarre had an issue with a lot of girls at her school and was the victim of a few different forms of harassment, verbal and physical at school as well as online through her media crap like MyFace. Harley had closed out her MyFace account page but some of the people that had harassed her online had still found ways to bother her. Felicia had sent an uplifting email that she should stand tall and stay true and just keep to herself and to avoid many of the hateful girls she schooled with.

Rebecca explained most of what she and Felicia had discussed and how desperate this young girl sounded in her email and the video asking for help. Rebecca told me that she wanted to try to reach out to this girl and offer a chance to escape her situation and come join us at the farm for the next school year. There was a small part of me that had hoped Beck's idea was purely a dream and suddenly I was faced with the realization of how serious my wife was.

I finished up my conversation with Rebecca and let her return to work while I got to brushing Banjo. Banjos attitude turned from playful to relaxed as he sensed my mind changed gears. I was trying to really figure out what I was getting myself into. I tried to contemplate what all could happen, I played scenarios in my mind to have strange, troubled girls join us in our farm and farming. Sure the help would be nice and sure Banjo would just love to have the additional attention but this wasn't something I was going to be able to take lightly.

Banjo was aware of the emotions of both Rebecca and I and he was very attentive. The next day I made to trip over to see Sampson. Banjo was always happy to ride shotgun in my truck wherever I went. Banjo and I took two lambs to Sampson to put some grocery credit on my account and Banjo was always up for a trip, especially to see Sampson.

Sampson greeted us when we strolled in and most of the time dogs weren't allowed but I entered through the back door and Winston helped me unload the lambs and lead them to the pen shed for their last stop before the meat case. I chatted with Sampson and told him about Becks' upcoming ideas and I took to listening to my wise friend. Sampson was already in the market for helping others and his protege Winston was his; more than a charity, it was a friendship. I asked what his thoughts were about taking on troubled strangers from parts of the country and the risks of opening up my home.

Sampson was totally on the side of my wife and he knew that the best investment anyone could make would be in the future and the children of it. Sampson shared in the pain of Rebecca and I being unable to conceive and he knew that if Rebecca and I had children that he would be the adopted grandfather. Sampson was one hell of a man and his worldly view was truly appreciated. I admired my friendship in Sampson and there wasn't much I couldn't trust him with, except Banjo, if he dog sat I know I'd come back to the fattest spoiled critter I ever met. Sampson was a good man and I couldn't ever come up with anything negative to speak of him.

I tossed some concerns to Sampson that I had, I asked his ideas about what to do and how to handle everything I was suddenly facing with everything my wife had concocted. There was a lot on my mind and looking at the business end of everything, was overwhelming. Sometimes the tasks of the farm became daunting so it was a nice relief to run for groceries or just stop off at Sampsons and check in on the man. Of course Banjo loved every beef jerky laden moment of the trip.

I finished my business with Sampson and left he and Winston to take care of their business with the sheep I dropped off. Banjo and I loaded back up and turned our front bumper back home, Banjo was nose to the wind and I was only a little more at ease about what might lay ahead. The drive back from Sampsons' wasn't a long one and it didn't seem to give me enough time to contemplate everything that weighed heavily on my mind. I wasn't a father but I knew that suddenly becoming a mentor to young teens would require delicate handling. I always assumed that you learned as you grew when an infant showed up and you kinda figured it out through trial and error. If I were to take on teens; there would have to be a lot less error, especially with teens that already had tender emotions and what not.

To take teens onto the farm would require a lot of teaching and coaching in how to deal with life in general. Teens have a hard enough time in life, things are chaotic in the world and every time you flip through the news there's always a story about some vulture or scumbag preying on some young innocent child and perverting them. It's a sick world and many youths need good mentoring and guidance I'm not sure I have enough of to help. I settled into the idea of not having children, this sudden reverse of the notion was a shock and I was still trying to get a handle on everything.

I was comfortably back home and I lead all the horses back to their stalls and set in to start cooking dinner for the wife and I. Banjo often belly crawled across the kitchen floor while I was cooking, I suspected he thought maybe he was invisible and waited to snipe in on some dropped food. This critter didn't care what was dropped, this boy has eaten potatoes, carrots, jello, grapes, broccoli, you name it, if people ate it, he felt intitled to a bite of it. I loved having Banjo and he was a great relief as a companion everyday.

Rebecca arrived at home and she and I sat down to eat, I was only half way through my meal when her mind overtook her self control and had to initiate the remainder of the earlier conversation. She and I spoke about the many risks involved with taking on other peoples' children and the many situations that might arise if we went through with this next adventure. Beck understood many of my concerns but her desire to help was more powerful than my hesitation. I told her about my meeting with Mike and she reassured me that Annie would help with the school paperwork as well as Felicia being able to help with the emotional needs of the young women.

I was still toying with many concerns and the idea of suddenly having my quiet farmhouse turn into a bed and breakfast. Rebecca was overwhelmed with the passion to help people and her passion was inspiring. Rebecca and I hardly slept but she had to work the next morning so I didn't want to initiate any conversation after midnight so we both laid there and stewed. I was ultimately nervous and she was ready to progress into her new dream.

"Help me, I am alone and have nothing left" Rebecca showed me an email she had received from Harley Navarre in mid-May. Felicia had forwarded Rebecca's email to Harley and explained what opportunity might be available if she was interested. Harley was from Beauford North Carolina, a small textile city not too far from the Capital and within an hours drive from the ocean. Harley was 15 and as a young lady she was backed into a mental corner by her peers.

Rebecca had exchanged a few emails over the rest of the month with Harley and had tried to gather as much information about the girl as she could. Rebecca told her about the farm and what we were trying to accomplish. Harley seemed interested in the change of environment but was hard to believe anything could change. Harley was depressed and prone to almost daily physical harassment or bullying from some of the older girls at her school.

Harley had a younger sister named Hattie that was still in the middle school and was starting to catch grief about her older sister. Harley hated the situation she was in and dreaded that her younger sister was heading towards the same fate that she was and that there wasn't anything that she could do. Harley was scared and everyday she woke up was followed quickly by panick attacks about the day to come. Harley had been suspended almost a dozen times for fighting and her parents just didn't know how to help her.

I asked Rebecca how she was planning to help, she just wanted to help so much but wasn't sure of how to even begin. Beck wanted to offer a hand but I was giving her reason and was prodding how she would go about truly helping. Could we as a couple emotionally offer help to fulfill this young girls needs and help her establish a sense of self that would carry her on through the rest of her life? Harley was excited about the notion of staying at the ranch for a school year, distancing herself from her environment and getting a fresh start but she was scared of so many things.

Harley had expressed concern for her younger sister, leaving her behind as well as the rest of her family and what would happen to her sister if she wasn't there to protect her. Rebecca had also been in contact with Harleys' parents Jill and Paul. Jill had mentioned that there was a major issue that had arisen earlier in the school year. The major issue that Harley had come into had really turned Jill onto that there were a lot more underlying problems than she had realized and that things had gotten out of control.

Harley had turned to cutting when the stress had flared out of control in her personal life. Harley had started using a sharp piece of glass to cut her arm, it was her only way of controlling anything in her life and at first had hid the marks under a long sleeve. One of her cuts had become infected and she ended up in the hospital because of it. After a weekend in the hospital; Harley had been committed to a psych ward and this lead to even more problems with some of the girls she went to school with.

Harley had lost the use of her pinkey and ring finger on her left hand as a result of her cutting and her self worth had really began to spiral out of control. Harley had the negative attention of a group of girls she had played volleyball with back in her middle school days and having lost all of her friends really bothered her. I felt bad for this girl and I'm sure it felt like her whole world was crumbling around her. Rebecca convinced me that this was a girl that needed our help.

Felicia helped to facilitate everything between Rebecca and Harley. Felicia was out as often as she could be to work with Elvis but she and Rebecca were good friends besides that. When the girls got together I was usually left to my own devices and toiled on my truck in the garage, Banjo usually sold me out, he was a traitor when the girls were around because he got more attention from them. I couldn't blame Banjo and I wouldn't mind the attention either but the jabber jawing grew old quickly and the solitude was a nice relief.

Harley was in dire straits and pleaded for help. Her initial plea was a desperate move initiated before she felt like she would kill herself. Harley couldn't take the abuse anymore and she didn't know what to do. I felt bad for Harley and wished I knew what to do. Rebecca offered to Jill and Paul to fly down to meet them in person and explain everything that she intended to do, or at least attempt.

I told Rebecca that I would go with her and that together; we would meet the parents and go from there. I wasn't sure what was in store but was certain that something had to be done. I was kept in the loop between Rebecca and Harley while Rebecca kept in contact with everyone in North Carolina. Jill and Paul wanted to do their best for their daughters but were at a loss for what else they could do in this media monster age. They were up against a world of teen monsters and many of them had no regards for their actions. I sympathized with Paul and Jill and wondered what good we could do if we took Harley for a school year and what might become of Hattie.

Rebecca planned a trip for the two of us in mid-June and I made arrangements for Randy to stay for the week and take care of the ranch. I was nervous about the trip but there was plenty to do around the farm as a distraction anyways. I tended to the sheep and sold off some of them and built up good credit with Sampson before we left. I scored another writing job in early June so I had to meet the deadline before we could leave. I had to write a manual for a new scanner machine that was being released to some hospitals in the West and they wanted updated instructions.

The summer was getting closer and Rebecca and I were enjoying the farming and gardening. She and I had a large garden plot and had a whole mess of plants to fill our kitchen with. I thoroughly enjoyed fresh tomatoes and usually ate my weight worth while I mowed the lawn. Rebecca loved pulling weeds and often did so while I was finishing cleaning stalls. The horse manure compost made for ample garden production and Sampson received many weekly deliveries of fresh produce for his store. I really had a good thing going with my ranch and I was nervous to teeter the delicate balance of everything.

Harley had emailed Rebecca and in strict confidence, had poured out how bad things were for her. She was getting jumped in the bathrooms at school, girls were pouring water bottles in her backpack, slapping maxi-pads on her back as she walked down the hall, making her a victim in anyway possible. Harley couldn't take it anymore and suicide seemed to be the only option she had left. Harley was frightened and without anyone else to talk to, she took to confiding in Rebecca. Rebecca was scared for Harley and I couldn't blame her.

Harley was an athletic girl, she played volleyball in middle school and was convinced against it before her freshman year started. As the year progressed, her social life spiraled violently out of control. High school is a hard enough time and most people make the transition with the help of their friends. Harley was the target of a few girls from her grade as well as the the older sisters of some of the girls so she was being harassed from many angles.

Harley was really struggling with everything she had going on and felt there was nothing left to live for. My heart ached hearing some of the letters from Harley and I knew that Rebecca was in deep need of having to help this girl. I worried about so many things and the only thing I could do was try to work out my thoughts while I worked on the farm. I had a hay cutting in late May, I had Mike and Randy to help me throw hay and as we made our way up and down the rows of cut and dried hay, I spoke to Randy about staying at my place and tending to things while my wife and I were gone.

Mike drove the tractor and he was left out of the conversation because he couldn't hear us anyways. I filled Mike in on the situation later that day over our ritual cold brews in the garage while Annie and Rebecca had the same conversation back at the house. Mike was leary about everything and wasn't sure how the adjustment would go if Beck and I were to bring a few young girls, with their own needs and problems into our environment and totally uproot them from their lives.

Randy was on board if there was anything my wife or I needed, it was his usual stance on life, to do the best he could and hope that it was enough. I confided in Mike and Annie about what was going to happen and that this upcoming school year was a pretty radical experiment. They both agreed but supported what Rebecca and I were planning to do and would also support the girls I was fortunate to have the friends I did and the support from them. Honestly though, I could drop some fruit in my looms thinking about everything and taking on such responsibilities was just scary.

Rebecca and I spoke about what would come this summer, Felicia would be out more to work with Elvis and we could have her help Randy with the horses so he wasn't overloaded with so much work and it would help us out a great deal. Rebecca would submit the idea to Felicia the next time she came out and of course, she was on board as well. Sampson was glad to help if he could but I knew he had plenty to keep him busy with his business but he and Winston knew that they could come get a lamb or two if his market needed them, I knew he would be fair and add it on to my account.

I kept a running tab with Sampson and at the end of each month, any time he was in debted to me over a hundred bucks he would cash me out and we'd start all over again. Sampson was a fair man and I had no worries about him shorting me, it was a simpler way of life and we kept it easy. Winston was a good help to Sampson and he was appreciative to learn a better way of things not to mention, stockpile cash for the upcoming school year. Sampson was pretty shocked that we were going though with this idea of Becks' but wasn't surprised that I was doing it, one of the soundest pieces of advice I received from Sampson and his worldly knowledge was to *"support your wife no matter what, if she's willing to spend her life with you, then spend your life with her!"* Sampson knew that I would be by my wifes side no matter what.

"I need help" Felicia and Rebecca found another letter posted on a social site in early June. This letter was from a 14 year old girl from Scotts Indiana. The girls name was Madeline Armstrong and like Harley, was being bullied and had no reason to live anymore. Madeline was in a worse situation than Harley in that she had tried to kill herself once already. Madeline was the victim of a group of girls that beat on her, cut her hair and ripped out chunks of her blonde hair in the hallways at school.

Madeline had chewed a bottle of aspirin trying to kill herself right before her mother Erin had found her passed out on her bedroom floor and rushed her to the hospital. Madeline was very agitated and desperate to change her situation. Rebecca went heart out for this girl just like she did for Harley. Madeline was a thin girl, a bit quiet and shy and also easily pushed around. Erin and

Rick are the parents of Madeline and like most good parents, they wanted the absolute best for their little girl. Erin wanted to help in any way possible and Rick was a construction worker so his mentality was to try to fix things with force.

I understood where Rick was coming from but Felicia explained that it wasn't always the best route to take when it came to dealing with the emotional needs of a young girl. These traumatic experiences reflected those of Kaylee before she passed away and it made Rebecca work harder to want to help. I was going to stand by my wife and any task she took upon herself she took onto the both of us.

Madeline was an only child and letting her go for a school year was very scary for Erin and Rick and there were many phone calls with Rebecca and I. Beck assured the Armstrongs that we would fly down and meet with them and explain our farm and mission better. I felt the sense of urgency in Rebecca's voice as she told me about Madeline; and like Harley, I wanted to help. I worked around the farm and tried to finish as many of my spring chores as possible before Beck and I headed out to fly back and forth across the country.

I was nervous to meet some of these parents and if I was going to be able to convince these people to let their daughters come with us or that we could offer more help than they can provide? I really felt bad and I realized that that was exactly what I was doing, convincing people that I could be a better parent, somehow. I was nervous and feeling guilty about everything and I would do it because my wife needed me too.

I enjoyed a warm Thursday with Beck working around the farm, we weeded, herded, and worked with our horses that we took pride in. I was at ease when I had Rebecca by my side and I could tell by her cute smiles when she looked in my direction, that my loving bride felt the same way. Banjo threw his ball around for himself to catch and chase after as he did when Beck and I were busy working with the animals. She and I then tended to the newer chickens and banjo was being a stubborn mongrel whenever we went into the pen.

I blocked Banjo from entering when I went in but that little turd burst in the door, bowling passed Rebecca when she followed me in, he barked and stewed up a mess of feathers as he ran back and forth and chased anything that moved. I must have stepped on a dozen damn birds and got pecked twice as many times as I lunged for Banjo too tackle his furry behind and wrangle him back out where he belonged. Rebecca and I laughed about it afterwards and it took us a few minutes to get the feed changed and things rearranged in the coop after the blitz attack by Banjo as the chickens were all in a huff.

Banjo was laying low knowing that he was in trouble and he often would go to the house and

face a corner when he knew he was in for a
scolding. Rebecca didn't have the heart to
reprimand the dog so it was up to me and I had to
do it. Banjo knew that the coop was off limits and
yet, the moron in him took over whenever either of
us opened that coop door and he just had to get in
there. None of the birds were any more than
startled but it was still a mess to say the least.
Banjo spent the rest of that day facing the corner,
his shame kept him from interacting with Rebecca
and I. Beck just felt so bad for him but it was his
own fault.

I tried to keep Rebecca focused on farm duties
but she kept wandering back to the situation
Madeline was in, she felt helpless that there were
such situations that caused girls to try to take
their lives, it was a sad situation that Madeline was
in, and in a supposedly safe environment like school.
These girls were cutting her hair and pulling out
handfuls, no student should be afraid to go to
school.

Madeline emailed Rebecca in early June as her
eighth grade year came to a close and expressed
her dread at starting her freshman year with a lot
of the same students that were horrid to her.
Madeline was willing to uproot herself and move to
another state for a blank slate and the possibility
of freedom from her mental prison. Rebecca and I
hadn't met with Erin or Rick but Erin was already
on board with what we were willing to do to help.
Erin said Rick was hesitant about sending Madeline

to our ranch for a school year and had many many
questions.

I corresponded with Rick and Erin and assured
them that everything was temporary and that this
was a trial situation. I kept note of many of the
questions that Rebecca and I got from the two
sets of parents and we did our best to come up
with the necessary answers. I still had a lot to
wrestle with mentally and I found comfort chatting
with Sampson when I stopped by and filled him in
on the latest news events. Sampson was a decent
listener and even when he didn't have a good
answer he still offered the best suggestions he
could muster.

Banjo and I worked around the farm, I took to
the four wheeler and he rode shotgun as we made
our routine search of the perimeter fence to make
sure there weren't going to be any escapee sheep
or coyotes getting in. The farm took a lot of
routine work and just general maintenance but it
was a pleasant routine and I enjoyed all of it with
my furry companion. I stressed a little at the
thought of having four teenage girls running amok
on the property; and having to host and all the
stress involved with that. I searched the fence
posts and wiggled them looking for signs of rot or
where wires had come loose from the sheep
constantly rubbing against the them

Madeline wanted a change, she wanted to
escape from her harassment and attempt to get a

chance at a normal young life, free of brutality. I often forget how cruel teens can be and that the lack of mental development can often inhibit kids from realizing the results of crap head actions. I always expected that as a parent I would be more interactive with my own kids and not neglect them to the point that they would commit heinous actions against other kids.

I felt terrible that teens watched enough TV that it numbed over enough brain cells to let them think that any of their terror was OK. I really worried that these kids were the same ones that might be running our country some day. The country has enough issues right now as people who have no sense of reality are suppressing the rights of those who pay their salaries. The world around us is a fly wrapped shit heap, much more sloppy than the manure pile I compost then spread on the hay fields.

I emailed Rick and Erin to see what kinds of interests Madeline had, I was curious if there was more Beck and I had to come up with to better host these young girls. Madeline was quiet and artsy, and like many young girls, the notion of working with horses was a pleasant idea. I wanted to help support the girls that were to become my guests and not just toss on a bunch of chores and hope that they earn their keep.

I warned Sampson that my food budget was going to increase dramatically and that I would probably be making more frequent trips. Sampson warned me that I was in for a whole mess of trouble, his son Freddie always had friends over and the girls usually ate like the men. Sampson wasn't making many things easier per say but he did lighten the mood. I ordered a handful of school supplies such as notebooks and any other things that Mike suggested I load up on for the high school curriculum.

Mike and Annie were a big help in getting us ready to take on such a large task. Annie helped to acquire the transfer paperwork and I faxed papers back and forth with the parents so that everything was legit. The work wasn't daunting but it was enough of a headache to wear me out at the end of each night. Rebecca and I managed everything together and I appreciated that she took on a ton of additional responsibility, even if this was her dream.

Rebecca and I had two girls essentially lined up to help. I was nervous to meet these young ladies and more than I was nervous, I was leary about what was to come. I had hoped that I could just trust them much like any other adult but I had to keep in mind that they were only adults in training and much like the horses, they needed love. I took Groucho out one morning and Banjo was in a piss-ant mood, he kept barking at Groucho and probably jealous that Groucho was getting my attention more so than he was.

I knew that Banjo would appreciate the
additional company and attention but I also worried
that maybe these girls had more emotional damage
than I could handle or Beck and I could help fix. I
rode Groucho, the light brown horse with black
mane, she was a big horse but fairly gentle except
for the quarrel with Banjo. Groucho took commands
well and responded firmly as she was supposed to.
I grew confident in riding Groucho and she slowly
got used to being a trail horse.

"Anyone that can help, I need it" Another email came in to Rebeccas' in-box. It was early June when this email arrived, this time the email came from the the western half of the country, in Arizona. Jordan Guzman was a 15 year old girl from a city called Gilbert, it's a suburb of Phoenix and heavy in gang issues. Gilbert housed a lot of sprawling up-and-coming neighborhoods and it allowed for trouble here and there.

Jordan was being raised by a singe mother; Corina, and Corina worked two jobs to keep her daughter on the straight and narrow. Jordan was an avid runner and not just to avoid the gangs that were trying to convince her to join up with them; violently. Jordan ran track and cross country and kept really good grades in school. Jordan was being jumped and attacked almost daily, she wasn't suicidal but she was desperate to find a way out of her situation and still graduate.

Corina instilled a hearty work ethic in Jordan and put stern emphasis on graduating high school, because she didn't. Gilbert had a decent school system but with the ever growing influx of families, they were often overcrowded and unable to keep a watchful eye on all of their students from one day to the next. Rebecca spoke with Jordan and Corina a few times and Corina was willing to let Jordan come spend a school year with us for the sake of her daughter.

Jordan loved the idea of banjo; a running partner. Corina was working two jobs to provide for herself and her daughter and it was almost too much and having a dog wasn't in the budget. Jordan wanted to escape from the harassment and knew that joining a gang would be the only true relief from their brutality but in the same respects, it would be her undoing as many of the girls from the gang ended up pregnant, in jail, or dead. I was excited to give Jordan the opportunity to be free from her bonds in the riff raff situation she was stuck in and even with her surroundings, she maintained a very focused head on her shoulders.

Jordan was hesitant on leaving her mother behind as Jordan was all Corina had. I was suddenly three girls deep in Rebeccas' idea and now things were getting serious. I was nervous about how everything was transpiring but it was getting to the point of no return. I loved my wife and regardless of what happened, we would get through anything together. I admired the passion Beck had within her and I knew deep down this is what she felt she had to do.

Jordan was an avid runner, she enjoyed the serenity of the warm weather in Arizona as well as the outdoors. I deeply suspected that running gave her a small sense of control in her life which didn't seem to have any. I was also curious if maybe the running came in handy when dodging the groups of girls trying to chase her down after school. Jordan sounded like she was struggling to survive at school but that her inner strength was admirable and because of it, she would persevere. I think adding Jordan to the mix would be positive. Jordan would be a strong role model for the other girls and a strong force that the others could take after.

I cleaned stalls and moved all of the horses out to their paddocks so they could run and enjoy the fresh air. Banjo darted in and out around my shovel and legs as I cleaned everything out. I refilled the stalls with clean hay and moved the wheel barrow along the center walk way between the stall doors and out the side so I could add it to the compost heap. Next was the less than ideal task of turning the pile over, I used my pitchfork to turn over the pile and in the mornings it steamed and stank of the decomposing road apples. Banjo kept himself occupied with some new found stick. Banjo was a good boy and as I had mentioned, he was a huge help around the farm.

I walked through the sheep and gave the necessary hand and whistle commands to keep Banjo engaged and move the herd to the far end of the second field. Banjo swooped back and forth and as the sheep scurried to avoid his heel nips. Banjo was well equipped to do his job as he was super energetic and fast. Luckily he was a smart breed and it served him well to do his job around the farm but if he wasn't worked often enough, he got himself into trouble. Banjo was a goofy feller and he was always doing something that had Rebecca or I laughing most days. Banjo was always nuzzling up closely and would use his snout to lift your hand every time you tried to rest it on an arm rest, he hardly gave you the time to rest without petting him.

I was glad to hear that Jordan would take to him and also run him. I knew that Banjo was going to truly enjoy the additional attention but I worried a bit about him, I really hoped that these girls were respectful and not mean to him for any reason. I was pulled in many directions and I had so many worries on my mind, fortunately the ranch had to many things that required my attention to dwell for too long. Even when the daily chores were done, there was buckshot to work on, my old truck. Banjo was much like a wild three year old and constantly needed supervision.

I tried to finish my newest manual in time for the week Rebecca and I set aside for our flight to North Carolina and then to Indiana. I was quietly thankful that Corina didn't need the face to face and yet; I wanted to visit Arizona more than the other two states. Beauford was forty minutes from Raleigh and Scotts was a farther drive to the southern point in Indiana. I booked our flights to leave Detroit metro, Rebecca and I would spend two days in North Carolina and three in Indiana. I was getting close on my assignment deadline but by the first week in June, I was confident that I would make it. I took the gamble and decided that I would postpone the hay cutting until I got back.

Rebecca took on additional shifts to cover her days off rather than use up her time off just in case some of the girls needed the additional attention during the school year. Rebecca was the department manager and she was a solid asset at the hospital and her coworkers were surprised but also very supportive of what she was doing. Rebecca had a very supportive group of friends with Annie and Felicia as well as a group of ladies from the hospital that she occasionally hung out with. Rebecca gathered ideas and notes from her friends with teenage daughters so she could be better prepared as to what to expect when these girls arrive.

Jordan corresponded with Rebecca during the remainder of June and she and Rebecca got along well. Rebecca was leary about how the school year would go. When parents enroll kids it starts out easy and continues to get harder each school year, we were going to get dropped right into the boiling water craw-fish style. Mike and Annie worked in the school system and were willing to help facilitate the paperwork and the girls' papers were coming through so there wouldn't be any hiccups in the transition, hopefully.

Sampson was having Randy do some work around his market, upgrading walk-in coolers. Randy was going to stay at the farm in one of our spare rooms and hammer out our chores and the tasks we needed of him while also working for Sampson. I dreaded that Banjo was going to be at the market all day long while Randy worked and I knew wholeheartedly that Sampson would spoil the snot out of that dog. Sampson was kindhearted and loved Banjo a whole lot and I couldn't fault Sampson, and yet, Banjo loved every beef jerky treat that came with it, spoiled bugger.

June 18th was closing in, Rebecca and I were gearing up and getting ready to fly out and her anxiety was growing as each day grew closer. Rebecca and I traveled on and off during our marriage and flying wasn't anything new for us but this was a new reason, it wasn't a vacation. Rebecca and I planned to eat out a bit while we were out in North Carolina, barbecue was fantastic and in that region, it was a dry rubbed style. Rebecca and I booked a hotel near Beauford and planned to meet up with Jill and Paul initially and then again the next night with them and their daughters.

After two days we would fly out of Raleigh and into Indianapolis mid-day. Rebecca and I figured we'd make introductions and meet and greets in June and then have the girls fly up to join us in early August. The last hay cutting is usually in mid September so the girls would get a good chance to cowboy it up and put some good work into the farm. The school year started the day after Labor day so it would allow the girls to acclimate to the farm and get familiarity with the chores that each would have to perform. Rebecca and I wrote out a list of tasks each girl would have to do but many hands make light work and with a few extra hands, things would get a lot easier.

June came upon us and the farm was teeming with critters. The baby lambs were still leaping about in the pastures, the chickens were still noisy and clucking away their days and the horses were as they were. Banjo could tell that Rebecca and I were up to something and he seemed a little more co-dependent than usual. Randy was beginning his work for Sampson but stopped out a few nights to make sure he had his lists straight as far as which horses got which mixes of feed and the routine of the pasture changes for the sheep. I also made sure Randy knew which commands made Banjo do what to better work with the herd.

Randy and I closed out a few of the nights with a few beers and shooting the breeze while I wrenched on buckshot, Randy just wrestled with Banjo and enjoyed the oldies on the radio. Mike met up with us in the garage on a Thursday night and his wife had joined mine with some mason jars of green apple sangria on the patio. The ladies just enjoyed the sound of the buzzing bug-zapper while the fellas and I just went over the lists I had to half keep my wits about me when my life tried to veer off topic.

The time to head out was drawing closer and as each day passed I seemed to work harder around the farm to keep my mind off the upcoming life change. I updated the chicken coop and made sure there were plenty of perches, I ran eggs to Sampson on my usual Thursday run for him to keep farm fresh eggs stocked in his cooler, I put down fresh shavings and hay in the stalls and re-stocked the hay in the loft so I didn't have to throw bales from the front of the loft to the back of the barn when I needed it.

I rewired the newer rat traps I designed. I figured out using a "Y" shaped chunk of PVC pipe that rats would enter the side while smelling the peanut butter in the upper lid, walk through the electrodes and get zapped then fall down the down facing hole and right into a trash can., it was a simple design and the few mice that landed in the trash can proved to me that the traps did well and never seeing any mice left me at ease that the horse feed wouldn't tainted with mouse crap.

Most farms have cats to chase mice and what not but most people don't realize how nasty the little beasts are. Cats are dirty little buggers and

I've met a lot of people that have been hospitalized from bites and scratches that are filled with bacteria and necrotizing diseases. I can't stand cats anyways and I'd rather rely on traps and my curious little dog to fish out any new smell that he couldn't get to. Banjo would go nuts once in a while, would try to dig through a wall or the ground and dig like a rabid mongrel and I'd know there was a mouse and find, it worked out pretty good.

Rebecca kept in contact almost daily with the girls that she semi-recruited to be her guinea pigs. I felt bad that I kind of looked at all of this as an experiment but I was leary about getting attached only to watch these girls go back home and to their lives. I've alway thought that life was just memories, some just hadn't happened yet. I was excited to see what kind of memories these events would lead to. I wasn't sure what some teenage girls might teach me but I was open to it... mostly.

Rebecca and I had everything we could think of straightened out before our excursion were to take place. I made sure Randy had what he needed and I had finalized the paperwork necessary to make my writing employers happy. There was so much to contemplate and even with the brain trust of our friends, Beck and I were certain that we were forgetting something. It wasn't a long drive to metro as we headed out on the 18th, Beck and I were going to miss Banjo and the farm and this was the longest we'd been away from him for anymore than a weekend. There was so much on our minds but so little on our lips. We rode in silence because one of our agreements was that we would organize our thoughts before speaking, no matter if it was while angry or just playing, we were both so jumbled with thoughts that silence was the only option.

We made it to Metro and as everyone hustled and bustled I made one last call to Randy and made sure everything was covered. Once on the plane and we were committed to the sky for the next three hours, Beck and I loosened up a bit, we spoke about Madeline, Harley and Jordan and how everything was going to turn out. Harley was going to be our first stop and I had a slew of questions. I remembered that Harley had taken to cutting and that made me slightly nervous because that meant she was possible more of an aggressive person and I had ample amounts of tools and equipment in the barn and garage. I chatted with my wife and we played out hundreds of scenarios and stuck to our guns and rehearsed our vows to one another; to be there for one another.

The flight wasn't nearly long enough but we were glad to be on solid ground. We fumbled our way through the airport and got our Ford rent-a-car and headed north to Beauford. Beck and I kept talking back and forth and tried to make sure we had any answers that Jill or Paul might ask. I was glad that Rebecca was a nurse and it has come in handy many times around the farm. Every time she held my hand, Rebecca was always fondling my arm with her other hand searching for a good vein for an IV out of habit. One time I sliced my arm pretty good on a shearing blade and Beck absolutely loved getting to put fifteen stitches in my arm. No I don't keep Vicro stitches around the house but e-z glide dental floss works out very well, and it's the country way.

Our drive to the hotel was pleasant and it was a decent place to camp out at for the next few days. Rebecca and I hit the hot-tub to relax after the cramped seating on the plane. Planes suck, you have to perform a lap dance to get in or out of the seat to go to the bathroom. I was nervous about everything and rightfully so, Beck was also. The hot tub was a nice change and we soaked for probably an hour as we kept talking about everything that was ahead of us.

Five o'clock came and we geared up for our dinner meeting. Rebecca called Jill to make sure everything was still a go and we settled up on an Outback Steakhouse in town. I was starving and hoped that we'd have plenty of time to eat while the four of us we able to talk. We made it to the restaurant at our designated six o'clock and cordially met Paul and Jill. They were both in their mid forties, had an easy going air about them. Paul rocked a monstrous goatee that came down to his armpits, Jill had long wavey brown hair twisted up in a butterfly clip and both were ready to eat also.

The meeting went well and we crossed many different topics including; insurance, the school year, Felicia being a school counselor, working with the horses and the other animals on the ranch. Both parents were very concerned about their daughter and we also spoke about Harley and some of the trouble that she had found herself wrapped up in during the school year. Harley was a bit of a fighter and very rough around the collar after an aggressive school year. Harley was a volleyball player in eighth grade and wanted to get back into it in her freshman year but social obstacles prohibited it from happening.

There were many concerns from Jill and Paul and understandably so. We suggested they think about it as a summer camp, but more so like a school year long style camp. We spoke about Felicia coming over on Sundays and that she would go trail riding with the girls for group gatherings and team building rides. We had miles of trails in the woods and there were plenty of horses for each girl to work with and ride. Each day would bring it's own chores around the farm and school work would be the highest priority but each girl would also be encouraged to participate in school activities.

Paul was hesitant to let his oldest daughter head off across the country to Michigan and spend a school year so far away. Jill was in tune with what Harley wanted and was willing to let her daughter make the choice, knowing that Harley was becoming an adult, making her own choices for her own betterment was going to be Harleys choice. We all finished our meals and said our goodbyes and parted ways for the evening. Beck felt good about the meeting and we discussed our newest thoughts and feelings about the ordeal as we headed back to the hotel.

Beck and I ducked back to the hot tub to finish up our day before going to bed. It had been a long day with the travel and everything. I sent a text to Randy to check in on things and his response was a sad one. Banjo had been moping all day long, he wasn't himself, he just laid around, no playing, no mischief, he missed us and Randy didn't know how to cheer him up. My poor boy was missing me and Rebecca and I wished I could do something. I suggested that the next day he feed the chickens and maybe hold tight to his collar and let him lick a chick. Randy just texted a lot of question marks about my idea but it was all I could think of to perk up my friend.

I thanked Randy for taking care of things and reminded him it was only for a few days. I professed my guilt about Banjo and Beck knew how bad I felt that he was having such a hard time. Rebecca and I enjoyed the hotel room and not having to be up with the break of dawn to clean stalls or run the gauntlet required to keep a farm running. This was a pleasant break from the daily tasks and frankly, I can't even remember the last time I was able to sleep in. My lovely wife and I joked and laughed away the rest of the night before succumbing to slumber. It had only been a few weeks but I don't think Rebecca had slept so well in a long time, her brain and heart seemed at peace once again.

The next day came earlier than I had planned. I was wide awake and ready to shovel stalls, except there weren't any, I guess my body was just used to the work so I snuck out and made my way to the hotel gym. I walked on the treadmill for twenty minutes and threw around some weights to keep up some cardio exercise. I knew that if I didn't work out some each day then I would be stuck with leftover energy at the end of the day. Around eight I made my way up to see if my sleeping beauty was ready to get up and moving. She was struggling to open her eyes as I opened the door but she instructed not to kiss her because her teeth felt "*mossy*."

I showered and cleared the way for her to follow my lead. We dressed and readied ourselves to go hit the local shops and stuff to spend our day before our second meeting with the Navarres.

It was time to officially meet my wifes younger pen pal. We met with the Navarres at seven at another steakhouse, this time a local joint. The pulled pork was fantastic and the cornbread was amazing. I am a foodie and everyone appreciates a good southern meal. Harley was a tall thin girl, she kept her hair fairly short in a bob style cut and she had light highlights in it. Harley was respectful but you could tell by her constant looking around that she had her ghosts. Hattie, the younger sister was beginning to catch grief in the middle school from girls that knew of the crap her older sister was struggling with.

We suggested that they tell people that Harley was in military school for the next year or with family, it wasn't anyone's business but using the military school excuse might buy her some credibility when she returned. Jill liked the

military school idea, teens aren't the most keen
when it came to propaganda and by telling people
the story, the girls could make up their own rumors
and maybe build up Harley with some made up
military training, it might discourage classmates
from messing with her when she returned.

Hattie was jealous of her older sister and was
going to miss her something fierce but she felt
that this was a necessary step for her sister.
Harley was scared to leave everything she knew
but it was better than her ideas of an escape.
Harley was slow to make eye contact and you could
tell she lacked confidence in herself as she walked.
The Navarres worked hard to provide for their
daughters and you could tell that they were both
lost as far as how to help their oldest and the
previous evening, Jill mentioned that she felt like
she had failed as a parent with the situation that
Harley was in.

We concluded our evening and the only last
questions they had was what was going to happen
next. Beck assured them that flying Harley to
Detroit in mid August was the tentative plan
between her and I and that we would get her ready
for school from there. We each shook hands
goodbye and Harley hugged Rebecca with a big
"thank you" and a smile. Everyone seemed at peace
about everything and Paul gave me a nod of
approval about our willingness to help.

Beck and I soaked one last hour before we went to bed that night. We had an early flight to Indiana the next morning so we also semi packed up our stuff. Rebecca and I laid in bed and spoke about how good we felt about everything. Beck was grateful that I took on this task with her and we fell asleep hand in hand. The next morning we hurried to make sure we had all of our belongings, our room tidy and headed back to the airport. We followed the route of the GPS on my cell phone and beck used hers to keep up on her emails. She sent messages to Jordan to see how she was handling being out of school and how ready she was to come join us in two months.

Jordan was excited to change her surroundings and have a school year free of gang pressure. Madeline sent an email explaining that she was looking forward to meeting us later in the day and Beck reassured her that we were on our way. Beck also emailed Erin and Rick to confirm that things were still on schedule for our group meeting. Beck and I only planned to meet the Armstrong's once on our trip but wanted to spent two days in the area to relax. I hadn't planned to do much while in Indiana and it wasn't known for anything special but a relaxing two days in a hotel sounded pretty good.

Beck and I weren't in our twenties anymore and the flight travel was rough, my lower back was not my friend right now and Beck was feeling pretty sore too. We returned our rental car and boarded the delta flight to Indianapolis. I checked my text messages and when I saw one from Randy I felt sad immediately. Randy told me that Banjo was still belly aching and even with the tease of the chicken pen, he didn't change much. I felt terrible that my little buddy was sad but three more days and I'd be home with him.

Our flight was like any other, cramped and uncomfortable. Beck and I made the same fumbling march of the penguins as we had two days prior to secure our rental car and get as far from the airport as possible. We headed towards Scotts but there wasn't a hotel in the small town so we settled on Evans, it was only 13 miles from our destination. Beck and I were worn out from the three hour flight followed by another two hour drive, with the hour time change and all the back and forth, it was hard to keep up with time. We stopped for lunch at some local diner and then progressed to our hotel.

The hotel was a dainty country inn but it had four floors and a pool. The hot tub called our names once again. We soaked for a bit and just sat there quietly relaxing. The hotel was almost empty that day, it was nice not to be splashed by unruly kids or engaged by strangers in the tub, my wife and I were able to just have quiet us time. I loved my dear wife and every once in a while I imagined what it would have been like to have brought our own child in to this world. I really felt bad for these girls and deeply hoped that what Beck and I were doing was for the greater good.

Beck and I headed back to our room and got ready for another dinner meeting. She called Erin Armstrong to make sure everything was still good and ready, both women seemed excited to finally meet. Erin was looking forward to being able to put a face with the lady that she had been frantically emailing with over the last month or so. Rebecca was ready to go before I was, which has never happened, but in my defense; she hogged the mirror before I could get to it.

We made out way to Scotts, it was a small town with maybe three stop lights. The school graduated under 300 students each year and each segment of the school system was located closely to the center of town. We found our way to the rendezvous point, a small mom and pop diner in their hometown. Rick was a thick built man, short hair cut and a rough short beard, he was a construction man and Erin worked in the school system. Erin was an average built lady with a vibrant smile and short sandy blonde hair. Madeline is a shorter girl, really meekly built and had long blond hair she kept brushed behind her ears.

We took a table and got passed our introductions. We started with some lemonades and some run of the mill chit chat. We ordered our meals and got to the heart of the meeting. Rick and Erin had a list of questions that they had written down and we all went through them one at a time. We informed them that the girls were free to come home whenever either party chose, that the chores weren't crazy out of control, that school work and grades were of the upmost importance and that respect all around was the second highest priority.

Rick spoke that he wanted his daughter to come home for Christmas and I set him at ease by informing him I would have no problems driving anyone out to the airport in Detroit at any time. Rick and Erin were very thorough with their questions and each of us seemed pleased at the depth of the information shared back and forth. Madeline sat quietly most of the time as it seemed to be her nature. I mentioned to Erin that the girls would be two to a room and it was for overall mental relief of the girls to have a roommate, confidant and also that no negativity among them would be tolerated. Madeline smiled a bit when I spoke about Felicia and the horseback riding sessions and that they would have access to the horses at anytime with supervision.

We made out exit after dinner was completed and all the questions answered. Beck and I were gracious that these families were willing to trust their daughters to us in hopes of improving the lives of their offspring. I felt at ease that night as I lay with my wife, her initiative and ambition to better the world around her, impressed me almost daily. I was a lucky man to have snagged such a

wife and I truly hoped to earn her love everyday.
We had a grand vision of a ranch, and a life full of
loving friends that we could grow old with and for
the most part, we had fulfilled our dream. Just
because one dream is achieved doesn't mean you
stop dreaming, life is memories strewn together
and each day you need to figure out what memories
you want to add to your stockpile.

Rebecca and I spent the following days in
Indiana just lounging about, Banjo stayed somber in
missing us and Randy did his best with the farm
but felt bad he couldn't improve the mood of my
furry pal. We headed back to Detroit and back to
our piece of heaven on the farm. Banjo was so
enlightened to see me and as soon as we pulled into
the farm he came out running and wagging the nub
that was once his tail. My best good friend was
back by my side and I his. I never let Banjo sleep in
bed with us but I suspected when I left for the
occasional business trip, Rebecca let him to keep
her company.

Randy was at the farm when we arrived and he
filled me in on the missed events, nothing to really
miss as things were mostly routine around the
place. I texted Mike and let him know the grill was
on at seven, I told Randy that he was expected to
join us as well. Randy joined me in turning over the
compost pile and after we got cleaned up, I started
some steaks and veggies for the grill. Mike and
Annie showed up with Felicia in tow, we all sat
around on the patio discussing how the trip went.

We talked into the night and portrayed circumstances that were ahead of us in the coming months. Randy had all but finished his detailed work for Sampson and Mike was preparing for the next school year already.

We had a great night of chatting and letting the blue light from the bug zapper get brighter as the summer sky grew dim and faded away. Every time I looked at my wife I was reassured that I had made the right choice in my life mate, and her smile let me know that she felt the same way.

July was teeming with the usual farm routine, shoveling stalls, feeding and brushing horses, and of course all the work with the sheep. Randy did a good job taking care of the farm when I was gone but as the summer goes on there always seems like there is more to do. I took to watering the pastures more as the heat increased so the sheep had plenty to graze. Rebecca and I took out the horses in different combinations to keep them used to being ridden and stretched.

Lemmy was still a stick in the mud and refused to lighten up but I was determined to keep on him and convince him that I'm more a friend than threat and that he can forget his previous life as a racer and enjoy the retirement. Rebecca kept in close contact with the girls we met as well as Jordan, whom we hadn't met yet. Each of the girls were still looking forward to joining us at the ranch

for a school year, Jordan had taken on a part time
job to pay for her plane ticket and to help out her
mom as best she could. Each girl had fairly
different backgrounds and upbringings but they
had many things in common as well, I hoped the
similarities would unite them a bit.

August came and we were within weeks of
meeting our new housemates. It was the second
when Rebecca got an email from Felicia, the email
was a forwarded desperate message from a young
girl that was in deep trouble. I was scheduled to
fly to Colorado for a meeting regarding my last
manual at a hospital to walk through it for three
days with a handful of hospital execs to train their
people on the new scanner I wrote about. Rebecca
had scheduled herself off from the 3rd to the 7th
while I was gone in order to take up the chores
that I would be unable to tend to whilst gone.

I flew out late on the 2nd and with shotty sleep
I was up bright and early on the 3rd in a conference
room to model the new functions. I was essentially
summing up my manual and had no real idea about
the machines I was talking about. I worked with a
man named Bob Curtain, he was a department
manager and a cheery guy. Bob had a crew cut hair
cut and his hair was white, he had a pencil thin
mustache and a very cherub like demeanor. Bob
helped me to set up what I needed in the
conference room and share some scenarios about
their work day.

I finished my first day in the conference room and Rebecca took care of our farm. Beck called me after my first training seminar and explained that she had found a very distressing post from a girl named Prestly, Prestly was 15, being cyber stalked by some creep that originated online and with a series of scary situations, she was ready to kill herself if something didn't change. Beck was full of sadness and emotions when she called me and I just felt terrible that I couldn't do anything from across the country. I asked Rebecca what she planned to do and she informed me that she and Felicia were already on the case. The two of them were trying to track down this girl and offer her the same help than was offered to the other three young ladies.

I paced my hotel room for a good hour trying to help postulate how Rebecca and I could help this girl but I was at a loss for what I could really do, I was committed to this training seminar with Mr. Curtain for the next couple days. Rebecca was stricken with the deep seeded desire to help people and I knew deep down if she didn't at least try then she would be haunted by the potential end results. I bid my wife the sweetest of dreams and wished her a goodnight as it was late for the both of us. I held my second seminar meeting going over updated and new functions for this new hospital device and dealt with the onslaught of questions and people fighting to stay awake.

Rebecca sent me a text and it popped up on my phone as soon as I was free from that hospital and into a world of cell service. I called her immediately and she shared with me her good news. After searching media sites with Felicia the entire day after chores she was able to locate an email address for Prestly Mills and she sent her an email. Prestly responded before I left the hospital and this poor girl poured out her guts and anguish. Prestly had been taken advantage of and the video was being used to blackmail her and things just spiraled out of control for her.

Beck insisted that she speak with the girls mother and be able to explain what was being offered. Beck told me that she wanted to fly to New Mexico that night and meet with the girl and her mother and be back around the same time as me. Felicia used her frequent flyer miles to fund the sudden trip so Beck didn't have to pay for the whole thing. I was nervous about Rebecca going on her own but she was a big girl and I trusted her decisions., this was something she had to do.

Beck flew out and met with Prestly, her mother Emily and her father Jim. Beck said that her parents didn't have a whole grasp at how severe things were, there wasn't a lot that Prestly shared about it all with her parents, and understandably so, but we encouraged honesty. I waited up for hours for the phone call from Beck to get filled in and I was a wreck. I wanted to be with my wife and I knew this was her dream but it was my responsibility to be by my wifes side and have her back. I found the link on my laptop to look up the post that Prestly had posted to one of the MyFace sites and asked for help.

Rebecca called and explained the entire meeting. I knew the meeting was a wrought with pure emotion much like the post was. The post said that she was in deep trouble and had no one to turn to and that she was scared and didn't know what to do. Rebecca stepped in and offered a school year with a fresh start. Prestly was fondled and too afraid to stand up for herself and push to press charges. Prestly was backed into a corner so bad that she had considered suicide and after seeing so many other girls take their own lives all over the news, she figured out the what and when of it all. Becks' email of help came not a moment to soon and it took some persuasion from Beck but her parents were on board and Prestly was willing to do anything.

I flew back to Detroit and called Randy to let him know I was on my way home and how I truly appreciated the emergency coverage. I made it home before my wife and I loaded up some sheep for Sampson, Randy passed on the message that he placed an order and I needed some groceries anyways. I headed to Sampsons to chat with him a bit, I filled him in on the latest fun in my life and he just played with Banjo mostly. I was really worried that if any of these girls got really desperate and tried to kill themselves that I would feel terrible, but what toll would it take on my bride? Could she handle someone that she had bonded with taking their life again? Kaylee was her younger sister and best friend when everything happened and it really twisted her up for a long time.

Sampson was a good man to talk too and he had ample wisdom about life. Between my plane time, her plane time and the days' work, I hadn't heard from Rebecca much and frankly, it sucked. I texted Felicia and asked her what her part was in all of this, she was talking with Emily and Annie and trying to expedite paperwork for Prestly to enroll in school as well as make other arrangements that might be necessary. I was thrown a wicked curve ball with all of this and all I could do at the moment was stick to what the farm needed and wait for my compatriot to make her way back home.

I bid Sampson and Winston good days and loaded up my pup and we raced back home, hoping Rebecca would be there. I hadn't even unpacked, I had dropped everything in the living room and headed to Sampson's' with his request. Rebecca still wasn't home by the time I arrived but her call came through shortly after and she spoke her entire drive home with Felicia driving. Prestly was a beautiful brunette with long hair and a petite frame. Prestly hadn't explained much at the dinner meeting I guess but from what Emily spoke about, things were in poor shape within the home because of it. Jim was angry that things had become what they had and he wanted to rely on his past military experience to just brute all of the nonsense away.

Jim was hard to comprehend how teen girls worked, he wanted to stand firm and do anything possible to make his little girl all better. Beck explained to him about some of the other girls and the slew of situations that have become common place around the country. Rebecca sat with Jim and Emily for a long dinner, with Prestly in company. Rebecca told the trio about everything that could be offered and the rules we are stern about around our farm. Prestly understood the chores and about the school work, she wanted so desperately to be away from the people that knew her demons and tried to exploit her. She was on edge and hadn't slept for a while but didn't want her business shared all over town anymore than it had already been.

Rebecca told her that the problem was going to remain the same problem but the only variable she could change over the course of the school year was her ability to be resilient about everything. Beck explained Felicia's role and how the team building should go. Everyone hoped that by working with Felicia and with a clean slate for a school year that things would be easier to stand up and face once she returned. The notion of being able to pack up and run to a foreign land, or state rather, was something each of these girls need and we had the ability to provide it. I had hoped that these young

women could grasp what they needed too in order
to flourish and grow into sturdy young adults.

Rebecca and I worked our hind ends off to get the house ready for the coming company. Randy helped me to build bunk beds for the two rooms that would each have two girls staying in it. I had three empty rooms but one was essentially storage and the other two were offices for Rebecca and I, we combined our offices into a corner in the basement and organized the basement to have a gym and the office as well as the large portion for storage. Our house felt like a beehive with the three of us working most days. Banjo didn't know what to think of everything, he just stayed hidden behind my recliner and stayed out of the way.

Rebecca and I were excited that the arrivals were coming sooner each day but also getting hit with the realization that these girls' lives were going to be in our hands for the next nine months or so. Jordan and Harley were due in on August

13th and Madeline the next day. Beck and I planned
to wait for them in Detroit and once we had the
flight numbers we were waiting for, we were off
and running. I wanted to take Banjo with us and he
seemed very sad that she and I were leaving him
behind.

Rebecca and I hung out at a waiting lot with a
line of cabs as we waited for Harley first, when
time came we headed to the long line of off
boarding passengers and I ran in to find the young
lady and help with luggage while Beck waited in the
car, Detroit is nasty in that if you exit a car, even
to load luggage you get nailed with a ticket for
standing or some nonsense. I located Harley and we
made conservative greetings and headed to the
luggage coral.

Harley said that her flight wasn't bad but her
nerves were a little rough as this was finally coming
to fruition. I let the two girls hang out in the front
seat and get acquainted while we waited the next
hour for Jordans flight to land. There wasn't
enough time to drop Harley at the house and it
would have been senseless to do all the additional
running anyways. Harley was fairly quiet and timid
with all of the changes. I planned to have a cook
out when everyone was settled and at the farm and
had a bigger one planned for the following night to
include the new guests as well as Mike, Annie,
Sampson, Randy, Winston and Felicia, it was about
to become a giant gathering having everyone at
once.

Hosting was a bit of work but it was always nice to have good friends all gathered around and on a nice summers night. We went through all of the mess of picking up our last passenger and once again I tracked down our newest guest and loaded her gear into the back of Becks car. Jordan made introductions with Harley and we all became more social on the drive to the farm. Jordan was geeked to meet Banjo and Harley was still semi quiet as she was unsure about the new transition. Beck and I rode in the front and took deep breaths to prepare us for what we had gotten ourselves into.

We pulled into the farm and once at the house we gave the appropriate tours so the girls could acclimate. Banjo was more than excited to have guests over and Jordan was just ecstatic to get to meet the boy she had heard about. The girls settled in and Beck checked her email to get an update on Prestly and to make sure Madeline was all set to meet us the next day. Prestly was scheduled to fly out of New Mexico two days after Madeline was set to arrive so she would be a bit of a straggler in catching up with the other three girls.

Jordan and Harley were given tours of the farm and introductions to the horses after the house tour was over and they were settled into their room. Harley kept her short brown hair out of her face with blows of air and it sounded like the horses a little. I showed the girls where most of the things were located that they would need for their chores, I also explained about the up coming hay cutting and that they were about to get a crash course in being farm girls, and quick. Harley was unsure about the whole throwing hay thing and Jordan was more ambitious about the task. I told them that Beck was going to run them through a few more ideas we had for them later.

I started getting things ready for the cookout and Beck had the girls helping out in the kitchen and explained whom the others were that would be joining us. Beck planned to take the girls to Tractor supply to load them up with farm gear so they didn't wreck their own clothes while shoveling and throwing hay.

Mike and Annie showed up and greeted each girl accordingly, Felicia was close behind and I got the food fired up. We feasted on plenty of grilled veggies and chicken and the girls ate their fill and socialized with the adults. Mike and Annie talked about the school and what they would have to expect when the year started out. Harley came out of her shell better and this time, the chatty Jordan closed up a bit. Harley was invited to try out for volleyball and Jordan was already planning to take up her usual running before the school year even began.

The night carried on and everyone got along very well. Once the guests left for the evening we all tucked in for the night. I was glad that Beck had taken the time off the help situate the girls in their new environment. 6am came and it was a bit of a habit change to have to wake the girls up and then get them started on their chores. Rebecca and I each took a protege and showed them the ropes of working with most of the horses. Harpo nailed Harley with her quick whisper behind the ear and Harley near wet herself and blurted out some unkind words, leaving the rest of us to laugh recklessly.

Harley toughened up and got to shoveling, Jordan was a little queasy at first shoveling the stalls, Harley fought for a minute to get a glove on and her temper almost got to her as she wrangled on a glove over her two fingers that didn't cooperate. We all led horses out but we had the girls stand clear as we took Lemmy out, Harley instantly knew the name as her folks Jill and Paul were more of the metal types; Jordan didn't get it and was really nervous to work with the horses.

We finished our morning shores and I asked Randy to join Rebecca in retrieving Madeline from the airport so I could stay at the Ranch with Jordan and Harley. I was tempted to take the girls out on some horses but wasn't sure they were confident enough with the large creatures yet to do so. I loaded up the girls onto my four-wheeler and gave them the extended tour around the perimeter. Banjo rode on Jordans lap and Harley kept a hand on him the whole time. Jordan was intrigued to run the horse trails with Banjo when there was time and I gave her my blessing.

I warned Jordan that there was the occasional coyote and she should only run when it's mid day, not near dawn or dusk as that was when they were more active, that's the biggest reason I barned the sheep overnight. I kept the girls by my side when I commanded Banjo to run the sheep and spread them out in the first pasture, both girls just laughed at how Banjo swooped and ducked back down at each hand gesture. Harley laughed as hard as she could be at the sheep hurrying to avoid Banjo and his nipping.

Jordan watched my hand commands closely and mimicked a few of them. I told the girls about training Banjo and that he was good at his job. Jordan was enthralled about Banjo and looked very forward to getting to spend time with him. Once the sheep were taken care of we filled the water buckets and troughs for the horses and shortly after I got the text from Rebecca that she and Randy were on their way back. I told my new house guests that the newest addition was on her way. Once Prestly was settled in, in a few days we would all be out grunting and cutting hay.

Harley was a bit more of an aggressive girl and ready for the hearty farm work, Jordan said that as a runner she wasn't foreign to getting sweaty so she was interested in learning the job. I hatched a new plan to make the cutting a faster task since I had doubled my work crew. Madeline made it to the farm, she was really quiet and shy, she opened up a bit to Banjo but avoided eye contact with everyone else. Jordan was outgoing and did her best to welcome the younger girl, it took a while and she managed to keep her long blonde hair tucked back which I took as a willingness to interact.

The bigger cook out went without a hitch. Sampson took to his Lou Gossett Jr. Persona and he and Jordan competed to out spoil my trusty four legged companion. Harley spoke about cars and wrenching with Randy and everyone got along fairly well. Rebecca and I loved having ample people to entertain, Madeline stayed quiet and mostly stared out at the horses kicking up dirt in the Paddocks most of the afternoon. I planned out the hay cutting with Mike and Randy as they were my trusty workers and together we would crew these green girls and put them to work. The girls heckled away a few hours and did well at making Jordan and Harley welcome while trying to engage Madeline, she was intentive but still very reserved.

We all spoke for a few minutes about the lagging arrival Prestly and we went back over the rules of the farm, be respectful and honest and keep things pleasant and polite. Harley still kept a bit of a chip on her shoulder, Felicia tried her best to explain to Harley that if she went into a new school with new people with an aggressive attitude than that's what she would receive in return. The girls all agreed to go into the new school year willing to try and leave their baggage behind them. Rebecca and I told the girls that if anyone of them went out for a school sport then some of their chores would be lightened up, we thought it might encourage them into the club activities.

I knew Harley was gung ho to get back to volley ball and figured Jordan was going out for cross country or track, she was a runner and it was her freeing talent. I worried about Madeline, she was eerily quiet for a teenage girl and by just looking at her, she seemed burdened by the weight of the world as she stared encompassing out at the horses. Teaching Madeline to work around the barn was as simple as it was with the other ladies and she was bright and quick to learn. All of the girls adapted quickly to their chores and I let a lot of my worries slip away.

Prestly joined us at the farm, she was nervous rolled in relief that her ability to flee her life back at home had come true. Prestly hardly had time to tour the home and get her stuff put away in the room she was going to share with Harley when Beck took them to get farm supplies. Each girl was given a list of things to get for themselves including overalls, a work shirt, boots and gloves. The girls all poked fun at the Carhart overalls and how stylish the duck browns were. There was a lot to do before the school year and we did our best to get them ready.

It was hay bailing day, I had the fields cut a day before so after drying in the summer heat it was ready to bundle and bail. I had Mike drive the tractor as he always did, Randy manned the wagon with Harley and Madeline while I had Jordan and Prestly help me stack the loft. Once the first wagon was full, I borrowed a Wagon from Robert Marion so I could leap frog while my team sent bales up the lift belt and stacked them neatly in the loft. I sent the bails up and the girls caught and stacked the bales. Harley got angry a few times, according to Randy, her fingers that didn't work made it difficult to catch and haul bales in quick pace as the spit out of the baler on the wagon.

Randy said Harley was "all sorts of pissed off" a few times and kept grunting and beefing through it all to make it happen. Madeline struggled with the bales that were almost as big as she was and each time she was knocked over, she quietly picked herself up and kept fighting the inanimate objects. I silently thought that the hard work might have been a rude awakening for the girls but that it would also serve as a bitter sweet learning experience to keep fighting, keep pushing forward and no matter what, don't admit defeat. A mans mentality was a bit more primitive for many things such as this but that it might also be good for the girls.

After the hay was all cut and stacked, the girls looked like a bunch of rung out dish towels, each of us were sun beat and battered but we men were a tad more used to this work having done it three to four times a summer. The girls had flung themselves upon the patio furniture and almost moaned in cadence with one another, except quiet Madeline. Beck had dinner prepared for after the hard work for everyone and we all cleaned off a bit in a hurry before we ate. After dinner Beck and Annie chatted with the girls while Mike, Randy and I played out our usual routine of a couple of cold beers as we laid around in the cool garage.

The girls retired one by one to shower and crawl their overworked bodies into bed as the sun slowly set. Madeline was the first to excuse herself from the patio, Harley and Prestly were probably to tired to haul their carcasses into the house till they were almost asleep on the chairs. The workout was a very good one and we each enjoyed the warm summer day. Winters were long and blustery cold in Michigan so Beck and I tried to soak in as many nice days as we could.

Mike rode off with Annie and Randy left right behind them leaving my wife and her dog-tired husband on the patio listening to the buzzing of the bug zapper. I asked her if she was worried that we had made a mistake, a truly bone headed mistake, like Metallica making an album without Bob Rock or ever having listened to Limp Bizkit. She was sure it wasn't a fatal risk like being an ICP fan or Westboro member; both of which should require sterilization, we chuckled at the quips we had come up with.

We remembered our agreement that we would do our best and that this was only a temporary situation that would hopefully have positive lasting effects on the young lives that were passed out inside. My wife dragged my worn out hind end into the house and Banjo followed closely behind. We still had a ton to do before the start of the school year in a few weeks. Banjo slept in the hallway to be near his new friends, I don't remember even laying down but the morning alarm came screeching bright and early the next day. Rebecca helped wake the ladies and we each ached and moaned our way out to the barn.

Beck had to work so it was just the girls and I to work. The tasks went pretty quickly with all of the extra hands and I honestly didn't mind the help. The girls chatted between themselves and helped brush the horses. I walked the horses out and let the girls get to work cleaning and freshening up the stalls. I told the girls that after morning showers and breakfast that I planned to take them to the school to get familiar with the new lay out and schedules for each of them.

We all loaded up into my truck, Banjo of course hopped in the back and kept his nose to the wind as we headed into town. Prestly asked me if it was even right to take him into the school with us but I wasn't leaving my buddy at home and certainly not in the truck. Banjo always forgot that he slipped and slided all over the place whenever he tried to run in the hallways but he quickly remembered to treat the smooth floors like ice. We met up with Mike and got a principal guided tour for each girl for their classes and around the building.

The girls each poked around and rehearsed their routine of walking between classes and stopping off at their lockers. Madeline was nervous that she was a freshmen and that she would be without any of her housemates in any of her classes, but it would make her step up and make friends. I discussed with the girls that there was to be absolutely no boys this year and that the girls needed to focus on themselves and their academic work. The girls all agreed that boys shouldn't be in the equation and we finished up our time at the school. We stopped off for lunch before heading back to the ranch.

The girls seemed to be settling in comfortably and nagged less about their chores as each set came and went. Jordan took to running the trails with Banjo by her side, Harley and Prestly lounged around in the living room and flipped through old Psych episodes while Madeline hid away in her room, I assume to draw of just enjoy the solitude. The school year came closer and closer and the girls voiced their opinions about dislike for riding the bus but I explained that it was part of the deal around here while I had to finish chores around the farm while they were at school.

Labor day weekend was full of barbecues and preparing the girls for their upcoming year. Jordan was excited to be able to wander around school without the risk of being jumped and harassed by groups of girls trying to recruit her into one of the Latin gangs that roamed the halls back in her hometown. Harley explained that she wondered how different it would feel to not have to worry about having locks of her hair cut while in class or be spat at walking through the hallways. Prestly was nervous about having to start all over but was open minded to the new environment. Madeline was insecure about what was to come but as a freshman was going to have to acclimate one way or the other.

The first day of school was upon us, each girl clambered about in the barn to get their chores knocked out before getting ready for their initiation into a new school with a slew of new students . The girls each primped and permed and my poor bathroom looked like a bombed out hut in Fallujah after they had all loaded onto the bus. I wished them all the best and reminded them all to remain open minded about anything that would come .

Banjo and I turned the compost pile and I took out Zeppo for a daily ride as we went around the perimeter of the sheep pastures. I always had to make sure the fences were tight and that the posts weren't rotting. The girls were due back around four so I started a large dinner and got all of the necessary supplies ready for all of the girls. I checked my email to see if there were any writing jobs that I could take up to fill my additional time. I cleaned up the house and got some laundry done for Rebecca and I and napped until the girls' arrival.

Banjo barked from his perch on my chest as we laid on the couch when the bus pulled up. I jumped to my feet to greet them and inquire on their first day in their new territory. Each girl ran through their day and it was positive for the most part. The girls spoke of favorite subjects and topics while I just listened. Each girl got their snacks and munched as we sat in the dinning room while Banjo belly crawled trying to be invisible while he waited for any potential dropped food. Madeline spoke a little that she dealt just fine with her classes, they all needed a few more days to become proficient at navigating the halls and the packed student bodies during the class transitions.

The girls joined me in working the herd out in the pasture with Banjo, each girl took turns giving him the hand commands to run the herds into the areas of taller grass so they didn't stomp or eat holes in one area too long. As the day toiled away each girl performed their afternoon chores and we cleaned up and waited for Rebecca to join us for dinner. Rebecca asked them each to rehash their first day and we did our best to take great interest in how things were going along for the girls.

Jordan signed up for cross country and I would make the runs to go get her each day after school as the girls finished their chores by themselves as the first few months went along. The girls took comfort in being trusted to work with most of the horses, except the stubborn Lemmy and they did pretty good at following the right mixtures of oats and vitamins for each pony. The girls cleaned out the horse stalls in the morning and the sheep barn in the afternoons. The complaining about the smells and waste piles from the animals reduced each day until finally it was just the way things were.

Jordan ran many, many miles, I took the girls to cheer her on during the local Saturday meets and we were each very supportive. As the Fall came and all of the trees in the area began to take on bright orange and red colors and then shat their leaves onto the ground, the girls became better acquainted with one another as well as with Rebecca and I. Each girl had a one hour session one day a week with Felicia at school and they all had their Sunday group session while horseback riding around in the woods together. Madeline was commonly on Harpo, the white horse with dark gray speckles. Jordan rode the more stern Groucho, Prestly on Zeppo and Harley on Chico. Each girl grew in their confidence while taking control of their large animals. The girls stood a little higher after a month or two on the farm as they learned their way around and what was expected of them.

Beck and I expressed our gratitude for the help and also our pride in each girl for how far they had each come since first arriving. Each girl seemed to blossom in themselves and continued to work to grow.

CH 12

The girls spent more time indoors as the weather turned sour. One Saturday was cold and rainy and the girls sprinted between the barns and the house to stay as dry as possible. I fired up the wood burning stove to knock some off the moisture in the living room. Banjo had rolled in some mud and was detained to the outer screened in porch, it was like his prison when the rest of us were inside. Halfway through dinner; Harley noticed the muddy snail trail that streaked through the kitchen and to where Banjo was rolling on the carpet in front of the wood stove, that little turd had snuck in to be by the fire and left a muddy trail in his wake. Madeline laughed really hard at Banjos' keen senses and how doing his belly crawl, this time, he had really become invisible.

Prestly and Jordan helped to clean the mess while Beck and Harley had clean up duty. I mopped the kitchen floor and Madeline took Banjo back to his cell and toweled him off. All I could do was shake my head at Banjos shenanigans and some days, his intelligence was more trouble than help. Each of the girls loved Banjo and that furry pest absolutely loved the almost round the clock loving. Our house seemed to breathe with all of the extra bodies and routines of chores and school. I moved both my desk and Rebecca's into the one spare room so the girls had a place to work on homework. Each girl kept up decent grades and worked together pretty well.

Harley spent some of her spare time in the basement gym, Jordan ran on the treadmill in her spare time also. I found Madeline sketching horses out in the barn and Prestly split her time in several different functions. As the weather continued to get colder and more rainy nasty; the girls grew a bit cabin fever like. Jordan and Madeline were roommates, I figured Jordans outgoing personality would encourage Madeline to open up more and maybe come out of her shell. Prestly and Harley bunked and seemed to have a similar interest in working out together.

I was barraged with girly chit chat and that wretched music of bass and some schlub that couldn't sing while the girls worked out in the basement. Most of the TV watched was a mix of Psych episodes and a few others. I forbode the reality TV shows as well as ones that portrayed girls in a poor manner. I wanted the girls to have positive influences and learn that a real girl should be self confident. Too many shows now a days had dizzy clueless girls with no skills or talent, galavanting all over the public because they may never amount to anything.

A sleeting early Sunday morning in November was an especially rough one. Tension had been rising around the house and you could tell the girls were starting to get annoyed at many little things. Harley still had a bit of a chip on her shoulder and had snapped a few times at the more cheerful Jordan. The girls started out bantering back and forth a bit when things quickly got out of hand. Madeline was mixing feed buckets and Prestly was leading Zeppo out to his pen after her and I put his blanket on him.

Harley verbally pounced on Jordan, Jordan let her pent up anger explode and lunged to put Harley in her place. The girls hit the ground and Madeline dropped an empty bucket when she was startled at the animosity. I lurched forward to separate the girls but between the hair pulling and screaming I was kinda surprised myself. I picked Jordan up and hung her by her overalls on a hook on one side of the center walkway and then had to stop Harley from lunging back by doing the same thing on a hook on the other side. The girls looked like pissed off pinatas dangling on those hooks while struggling to kick one another and exchange verbal assaults.

Beck was just outside the door with a cup of Irish breakfast tea for me when she heard the commotion, as she entered the door I was lounging back on a hay bale just relaxing watching our teen marionettes still gripe and moan. The girls still wiggled and reached for each other and also to try and finagle themselves off the the hooks that kept them suspended. Beck laughed at my cool outtake on the situation but realized that Madeline was on the verge of crying then she quickly walked to her for comfort. Prestly walked back in and asked "What the heck is going on in here?" This was a boiling point I knew that was looming over the past few weeks.

After a few minutes of hanging around and many complaints about "items" being wedged into the unknown; I reluctantly unhinged the girls and made them shake hands then shake off the aggression. Each girl muttered the apology and got back to work. Beck texted Felicia to come over a bit sooner as this group session was going to be a long one. I remained vigilant on the girls that were still hot under the collar and Madeline was still a bit shaken up after the events. Jordan was accused of having a raging "Latin temper" and Harley of being an aggressive "hillbilly chick." I tried to quell the tension as best I could but each girl was still pretty upset about being strung up like wet socks so they brushed me off as well.

I asked Harley and Prestly to restock the hay in the loft so it was all closer to the ledge and it would give Harley some additional work to help vent some of her hostility. Harley had a hard time throwing around hay bales because of her two fingers that kind of just stayed partially curled and refused to work on command. Harley had suffered nerve damage to the two fingers as a result of an infection from her cutting her arm, it was a bad decision and one that would affect her the rest of her life and she would have to somehow deal with that.

Prestly was still fairly willing to do anything asked of her but according to Felicia, still pretty reserved but not as bad as Madeline, Madeline was essentially closed off to everyone. Felicia arrived at the ranch and beelined to the Barn all dressed and ready to do some work. I asked beck to throw together a big thermos of hot chocolate and I turned up the heat in the barn where we would all powwow. Felicia told each of the girls that it was exposure time, time to spill the demons and be willing to trust that their secrets were safe. Beck came in with enough hot chocolate to go around and the girls each pulled up a hay bale, we didn't throw the hay in the stalls until after we were done with our seats.

Jordan spoke first, she spoke about the dozens of times having to defend herself or outrun different girls that were trying to jump her into one gang or another. She spoke about her many afternoons alone as her mother worked a morning shift waiting tables and an afternoon shift as some book binding company to make ends meet. Corina hardly had whole days off, she worked most weekend mornings and most weekday afternoons, her schedule didn't leave time to come to any of Jordans' meets or school functions and essentially, the girl has had to raise herself over the last few years.

Jordan has maintained a surprisingly upbeat outlook after all of the things she has had to endure to survive. Jordan did most of her own patchwork and cleaned up bloody lips or bruises, she learned most of the first aid firsthand. Jordan didn't know of any other way than to be tough and strong, especially when it came to fulfilling her mother's one request: to graduate high school. Jordan hid away after school and dove into her studies, she couldn't risk hanging out with friends and most of the girls she knew all joined gangs for protection anyways.

Jordan has known several girls that were raped, or beaten into gangs and all of them had ended up pregnant within a year of their initiation. Jordan was scared to death to go down that path and fail her mother. Shootings weren't uncommon in her area, she lived in an apartment complex for lower income households and that also housed many of the criminal types. In her neighborhood, even a lot of the thirteen and fourteen year olds were holding up stores and smashing car windows to prove their worth in a gang, and they all lacked the brains for anything else. Jordan dreamed of getting good enough grades to go to a decent school, not a community college, and get her degree in criminal justice, or kinesiology.

Prestly shied her eye contact when Felicia asked her to open up and share with the group. She asked if she could pass but Felicia was adamant that she speak. Prestly hung her head and cleared her throat before she started. "*It was summer after eighth grade*" she started out her conversation. Prestly said she was at a local pool when an older boy had fondled her through her bathing suit, she was scared and she didn't like it but she didn't know who the older boy was and with so many people it was hard to really be sure it was on purpose. As she entered her freshman year she noticed an upper class boy paying extra attention to her.

This boy had a scumbag name, "Terrance" he went by T.J. and he asked her out. T.J, was insistent that she go out with him, some of her friends thought he was popular so she buckled to the peer pressure. After a few movies over a few dates things really went bad, they ended up at a park one night and they had been making out a bit. It was getting sort of late when she had decided that it was time he take her home. T.J. slid his hand up her shirt and was grabbing at her chest, she described his rough hands on her skin and how much he was hurting her.

T.J. then described how much better her chest felt now compared to a year ago in the pool and that was when she lost it. Prestly said she started screaming and clawing to get him off of her and dragged her off of the big rock she was propped up on. When Prestly hit the ground it knocked the wind out of her, T.J. pulled her shirt up over her head and pinned her tangled arms to the ground and pulled out his cell phone. T.J. took some photos with his cell phone of her exposed chest and then told her that if she told anyone that he would show them to everyone she knew.

Prestly was trapped, she wanted to tell someone that she had been taken advantage of but didn't want her naked pictures spread all over the school. The blackmail got worse as the school year went on. T.J. then used his advantage over her to proposition oral sex from her a few times. Prestly described gagging and choking as he forced her down onto him. T.J. told everyone that Prestly was his girlfriend and her friends were jealous of her, none of them knew the truth.

Prestlys' situation continued through the school year and each time, she was told that she had better cooperate or her pictures would get out. T.J. took additional pictures of her going down on him and that forced her even farther into her spiraling world of torture.

It was Harleys turn to speak. She had tears in her eyes as she lived Prestlys' pain with her. Harley spoke that after last Christmas she had found some pleasure in cutting herself, she would use a broken piece of glass to cut lines into her left arm. The cutting hurt but the adrenaline that came with the drips of blood that poured out of her skin gave her a bit of a high. Harley said she would bandage up her arm after a few cuts and hide the marks under arm sleeves so no one would find out.

Harley back tracked a bit and spoke about going to a school dance in the previous fall. The dance was held at school and a few of her friends had scored some wine coolers before hand. The girls sipped the nasty alcoholic drinks but each put on a brave face in the front of the other girls in her group. One of the girls had an older brother that also went to the dance. The girls were partially buzzed and danced half the afternoon away.

Towards the end of the dance Harley was supposed to stay the night with her friend Aiden and her older brother Bastian. Bastian had a group of guys with him and they were secretly drinking whiskey and other assorted drinks during the dance. Bastian had convinced the girls to join them for an after party at his friend Shawn's place, there weren't any parents, and it was supposed to be a blast.

Harley said that she and her friends were excited to party with the older boys and felt older by doing so. Shawn and Bastian weren't the best students but they knew how to have a good time. Harley had never drank before but each drink didn't taste as bad as the previous and they kept the music blaring late into the night. Harley said she was beginning to feel sick and told Aiden that she might have had to much to drink and wanted to lay down. Aiden wanted to talk with Shawn some more and because he was friends with her brother, she had a bit of a crush on him for a while anyway.

Harley said she found a bedroom to sleep in and knew that Aiden was supposed to join her in bed anytime soon. Harley was beginning to doze off in her buzzed state when she felt someone climb into bed with her, at first she didn't think anything of if because she was suspecting it was

Aiden when all of the sudden a "SHHHH" came from a mans voice. Harley said she tried to scream when a hand went over her mouth and things began to get rough.

Harley said she felt her bottoms get pulled off of her and her top pulled up. Harley described the pain she felt in her downstairs and how she felt she was being ripped in half, some fabric had been shoved into her mouth and she felt the warm stinky breath on her skin as the man ravaged her. She didn't know how long she was victimized but as his energy wore out, another mans voice said "my turn" Harley tried to see who else was in the room but she couldn't keep her eyes open because her girl parts hurt so bad that all she could do was grunt away the pain.

The second man hooted and hollered as he pounded away at her pelvis, she could feel the man slide into her and the internal beating started all over again. Harley described the brutality as if it was happening all over again, it seemed as real in her mind as the hay bales she was sitting on. Harley said that after the second man was done they spoke about how fresh she was and their speak blurred in and out with her crying. The first man suggested that he wanted to go again and that the other should video the sweetness of her body and he wanted the night to never end. Harley said she was crying so hard and that she couldn't get a big enough breath to tell them to stop. Harley screamed out "NOOO" over and over as she was raped but that her screams went unanswered.

Harley said she felt like she was torn open and bleeding, the men pawed at her chest and it was so very painful. The second man bit at her neck and chest and the first groped her butt and inserted fingers into her. The mans finger nails felt sharp and she had a hard time telling pains apart in her body. Harley didn't know how long the assault lasted but luckily she blacked out from the pain as the second man climbed back on for his second time. When Harley woke up, her underwear was next to her head, she guessed that was her gag overnight.

Harley described the next morning, she stumbled to a bathroom and looked at her beaten body. Her delicate parts were covered in blood and other mess and she started a shower. Her head spun and pounded and she tried to wash off the stench of the two guys that brutalized her. Harley said that her breasts had bite marks all over and her face had puffy marks that were sure to bruise. Harley's legs were hurt and the in between was tattered and swollen.

Harley got back into her wrinkled dress and fumbled through the house to find Aiden asleep in the living room on the couch. The two men were no where to be found so she woke her friend and they walked to Aidens' house. The walk was painful as Harley had been forcibly raped, the walking was tortuous. Aiden was boasting on Harley about having become a woman with Bastian and how she was flirting with him half the night. Harley told Aiden it wasn't consensual and that it wasn't just him. Her head was foggy and it pounded like a jackhammer.

Aiden stopped walking when Harley mentioned it not being consensual, Aiden couldn't believe her ears and refused to accept that her brother had raped her, or that Shawn, the guy Aiden crushed on, had slept with Harley instead of her. Aiden called Harley a "slut" and stormed home ahead of her. Harley followed her home to get her clothes and then called her parent's for a ride home. Harley was in a bind, she wasn't supposed to be at a party, wasn't supposed to be drinking and definitely wasn't supposed to stay the night anywhere other than at Aidens house.

Harley found the trouble with her situation, her best friends brother had raped her and if she told anyone, her friend would never forgive her, her social life was ruined, her youth was tainted, she was screwed. She also knew that if she told her mother Jill that Jill would encourage her to do the right thing and that Paul would go homicidal and string up Shawn and Bastian by their boy parts and go all Silence of the Lambs on the boys. Harley was suddenly alone and had no one to turn to.

Shortly after the party, things had changed at school. The girls that had played volleyball with

Harley had turned on her, they all called her variations of "tramp" and "slut" and things like that because Aiden had told them all that she had given herself to Bastian when she was drunk. Bastian had raped her but was free of it and his little sister had sided with him; against her former best friend. Aiden backed her brother and had texted all of her friends what happened long before Harley had even gotten home.

The girls started off just raging on Harley but things escalated with the physical assaults as the school year progressed. One day in class a girl sat behind Harley and while the teacher had her back turned, she used scissors to cut a large chunk out of the back of Harleys' hair. Harley shoved the books aside and leaped onto the girl to pummel her, Harley was suspended for three days for fighting and was now labeled as a trouble maker.

Harley was stuck, any self defense she tried to protect herself with would support the fact that she was violent and aggressive. If Harley tried to tell the truth than she would be called a liar and people would make worse accusations about her. No one would believe that this fighting aggressive girl was such a victim and after a few days there would be no proof. Harley was the target of abusive little bitches and no one, even her friends, would side with her for the right thing.

I really got insight to how rough life was for these girls. Beck cried knowing that her sister went through a lot of the same lonely feeling before passing on. I was just taken aback at all of the information that was coming out of these girls, everyone was either crying or misty eyed and Felicia kept clearing her throat and trying to calm each girl. The barn warmed up as the afternoon passed, I suspected each girl was getting as hungry as I was but this was a solid session and the girls were finally unburdening themselves onto one another.

Being subjected to so much violence explained why Harley had such a chip on her shoulder, that paired with the traitorous acts her friends all committed against her, trust was hard for her to manage. I really hoped that by sharing their pains that the girls could each find a way to overcome their challenges and find a way to move on.

Madeline blew her nose a few times and then raised her head to take the clue that it was finally her time to speak. She tried to look around but still avoided eye contact. Banjo stood up and walked over to her and laid down at her feet to comfort her. She started talking but her voice was meek and she had to clear it a few times to make it audible.

"I was six when things started to happen" she began. She had an older cousin that lived a few doors down from her. Her cousin Charlie was thirteen and watched her during the summers while her parents worked. Her dad Rick worked

long hours in construction and Charlie was with her a lot. Charlie was a good friend at first and they played hide and seek, swam in a small pool and toyed in the sandbox. Madeline said that at first Charlie would have her change into her bathing suit in the living room while he kinda peeked at her and it only made her a little uncomfortable, but didn't pay much attention.

Madeline didn't know to suspect anything weird, it was her cousin and she trusted him, he looked after her. As the summer went on, Charlie would sometimes change into his bathing suit when she did, as they would watch each other. Madeline was warned by her mother Erin that boy parts were different than girl parts and that girl parts were private, she thought she meant to anyone but family because Charlie watched her change all the time.

The first summer it was only Charlie watching her change into her bathing suit and he watched her change from time to time. Charlie was over a lot after school during the school year until Erin came home. Charlie told her once that as his friend she wasn't allowed to tell anyone about their changing time and that best friends kept secrets.

The next summer Charlie watched her, things go worse between them, Charlie showed her his parts and that he was starting to develop hair in his private area. Madeline said she didn't want to see his private parts but he grabbed her hand and

made her touch him while he shook his penis.
Madeline just wanted to go swimming and he told
her she had to so they could hurry up and get
dressed in their swimsuits. Madeline was always
instructed to listen to Charlie and that he was in
charge so what could she do?

Things went on like that a few times, Charlie
then told Madeline that since she got to touch him
that it was his turn and that it was only fair.
Madeline said she really didn't want him to touch
her but she didn't want to be unfair either. When
charlie touched her he rubbed against her
downstairs and his penis stood up when he did it,
he had to show her. Madeline said she was weirded
out when her cousin showed her his boy parts.
After a minute or two of being touched, Madeline
turned around to get her swimsuit on while Charlie
heaved and shook for a few minutes.

Felicia's' mouth just dropped open but she was
unable to speak. Madeline was embarrassed to
tears and her crying got worse. Harley was closest
and she stood up and embraced her friend. Beck
spoke up and with tears streaming down her cheeks
she told Madeline that none of this was her fault.
Madeline started speaking again and told the group
that sat silently, other than the weeping, that the
following summer was the last that Charlie watched
her but it was the worst one yet.

Madeline spoke that the next summer Charlie
was working out and liked to go to the pool more to

look at the other girls his age and show off his bigger upper body. One day after there were three or four teen girls at the pool that when they changed out of their wet swimsuits that Charlie insisted she touch his penis. Charlie used his hand and wrapped it around hers to shake his penis and she just kept her eyes closed the whole time, he used his free hand to fonder her privates. Madeline was horrified after all was said and done because something warm and sticky landed on her bare chest and stomach that he had to wipe up for her afterwards.

Madeline said that after a few swim sessions that ended like the bad one, Charlie convincer her to lay down so they could touch parts and see how it felt, once again she ended up with sticky goo on her stomach and Charlie had to clean her up afterwards. Charlie continued to remind Madeline that friends don't tell and if she didn't do as she was told that he would tell her mother and that she would get in trouble. Madeline was in her own hell as a little girl and was being victimized by her older cousin.

We all sat in awe of this thin girl that had such a tragedy buried deep behind her shy exterior and it completely defined who she was. I tried to keep an eye on the speaker but not to the point that I was leering. My head spun trying to comprehend everything that had happened to the girls in my care. I wanted to hold my wife and convince myself that none of this could be real. I was sickened by my own gender for the actions of so many.

Madeline said the third time she laid down for her cousin he "poked" her privates with his own and it hurt so bad that she screamed and cried. Charlie shushed her and jumped off of her while apologizing for hurting her. At the time Charlie seemed scared that he hurt her and offered her candy and toys not to tell anyone. Madeline said she cried from the hurt for a while as they watched "Animaniacs" together.

When Erin got home Charlie did all of the talking for her, he said she had told him that she was getting a bit of a rash on her downstairs and that she said it was beginning to hurt. Erin told Charlie that it was probably irritated from the chlorine and that she'd put some ointment on her later on. Madeline said that her mom applied a cream to her bits and didn't ask any questions. Erin suggested to Charlie that they steer clear of the pool for a while and that was the last time she ever went swimming.

Madeline had one hell of a struggle to have to overcome and I truly had no idea how to handle everything I had just learned. I ducked out to whip up the late lunch for everyone and Beck brought everyone in to eat shortly after. I made beef stew with plenty of rolls and biscuits to complete the hearty meal. Prestly piped up that such a big batch of meat and potatoes might cause her to gain weight but I assured her that with all of the work and the upcoming cold weather that they would burn off any worrisome calories.

We finished the group session in the dining room, Felicia spoke to each girl that they had to be able to somehow accept what had happened to them and be able to forgive themselves. The events that each girl had endured must have been absolute agony and I truly hoped Felicia would be able to help them each to heal.

I silently wondered if Felicia knew what she was doing throwing a rock into the mental ponds of these girls and causing all sorts of painful ripples. Each girl had spilled their guts and no longer had to feel like they were alone in the world and could now confide better in their roommate, or Beck, or even me. My phone rang, breaking up the somber mood in the house, it was Sampson asking me for a pair of lambs to stock up for the week, I assured him that I'd be there within the hour with his order. I took notes of what each person wanted in regards to items from the market. I put my list in my pocket and headed out to load two lambs into my truck. While dragging the sheep up a ramp and into the bed of my truck, Harley came out and offered her company to go. I told her she was more than welcome to join me but she might not like the reason I was taking sheep anyways.

Harley said she understood the purpose of the sheep and even though it was a little sad, that's how life was. Harley was biting at her lip a bit then used her good hand to let herself into the passenger side of the truck. We headed towards the market and it was strange having a two legged passenger. Harley didn't wait long after we left the gate when she started talking. Harley aked how private the conversation really was, I assured her that as long as she didn't started cutting again that I had nothing to share with anyone. Harley then proceeded to ask more of her concerns

Harley wanted to know what might happen after the school year, what would it be like returning to her home life, how was she supposed to handle everything and if she even had to go back home. I tried to answer everything as best as I could, I warned her that one of the biggest tasks to being an adult is having the confidence in herself that no matter what was ahead of her, she would have to face life on her own. I explained that even though I had a wonderful partner in my wife to travel through life with that inevitably, we had to do it alone while together. Harley shot me a sideways look about the "alone together" comment, I tried to explain that I meant that even though she was my wife and I her husband, it was up to us to trust that person with out hearts and every little piece of dirt from our past.

People can be insecure, jealous and very petty if they thought too much about things in a negative way, I had to once in a while force myself to focus on all of the good that I had with my wife and keep in mind that she chose to be with me just as much as I chose to be with her. Beck knew me in and out completely and it went beyond trust, we could see futures with one another and honesty was of the upmost importance. We arrived at Sampsons, pulled around back to the small holding shed he had for the animals, then I rang the delivery bell to let him know that I was there. Sampson popped out of the door to greet Harley and myself and helped me to unload his order.

I handed the shopping list to Harley and sent her inside to get started on gathering all of the supplies we had to pick up. I sent Harley in to navigate and figure out as much as she could without any help, a small task sure, but another opportunity to gather a stronger sense of self. I parked back around front and went in to find the girl that came with me. I headed down the right side and made my way to check in with Winston at the deli counter, I asked him how he was doing and how his plans for the next school year were coming along. Winston had started online classes so he could make some progress and get some pre-req's out of the way. Winston wanted to major in accounting as he liked numbers and helping Sampson with record keeping reawakened his unique talent.

I watched Harley trounce up and down the isles slowly filling the cart with the items from her list, I could have gone to help her but I asked for most of the meat supplies I remembers that we needed. Sampson came out with a small list of what the newest addition of sheep and eggs would add to my running tab with him and I was sure that with my increased food requirements that I might be indebted to him for once. I suggested that if Sampson missed paying me that he could cut me a check for old times' sake, Sampson raised an eye brow and simply said "boy all that estrogen must be causing hallucinations." I did my best to keep a stern poker face but half a second after Winston started laughing, I had to join in. Winston was a sharp kid, he wrapped my meat order and Harley caught me shooting the breeze as the meat was at the end of her list and she wandered to the counter I was easing against.

I wandered with Harley to the checkout to finalize our order and saluted Sampson a farewell. Harley and I loaded up the food in the back seat as it was still nasty and drizzling. Harley asked a few more questions as we rode back to the ranch, she was intrigued how she was supposed to rejoin her life back in Beauford and all I could offer was no matter what, to stick to her morals and not back down, I'm sure the heat that she left behind would settle down with this passing year.

I can't say Harley was set at ease with my advice but I hoped it might give her something else to think about. We carried our supplies into the house and the girls helped Beck and I put everything away. I remembered what Sampson told me about young girls eating, that man sure wasn't kidding, half a dozen bags if chips a week, more veggies than I fed my horses and a large number of other snack items. The girls each called and spoke to their families on a weekly basis, Rebecca often took the tribe out on Saturdays for light shopping or hair errands and what not. I didn't mind having the house quiet with my companion for a few hours at a time. I had time with Banjo during the week but he often napped before he ran back and forth between them all to get maximum attention.

November was drawing to a close and I made the appropriate phone calls and arrangements for the usual giant meal. Sampson couldn't make it this year as his son Freddie and daughter-in-law were scheduled to fly up from Texas to eat with him and Winston. Randy was going to be eating with Mike and Annie but Felicia was a confirmation to join us. Prestly and Harley wished they could go home and join their families but they already planned to fly home for the Christmas break. Jordan worried about her mom all alone back in Arizona but knew that this break would save her some money and maybe even give her a break from the stresses that being a single parent came with.

Madeline spoke with her mom and dad but was still pretty mum on the situation from her childhood. The girls all did well in their academics and volleyball was set to begin so it was Harleys turn for after school specials. Thanksgiving came and all of the girls helped out as we prepared a massive gathering for the four of them, the two of us and Felicia. Banjo was frantic with all of the cooking and ready to attack any food item that hit the floor, he was funny about it. The girls all seemed to handle the holiday away from their families and the session in the barn that started with Jordan and Harley trying to rip one another apart hadn't come back up. Felicia changed her

group sessions to just doing chores in the barn
when ground was to sloshy to ride.

The holiday ended with everyone sprawled out
on couches or the floor, breathing heavily from
being over stuffed, Banjo got his usual large chunk
of turkey with a little gravy on top and he was on
his back near the fire place, it actually seemed like
he was too full to be petted which was unusual for
him. It was comforting to have a room full of
people and my wife snuggled up at my side. I knew
we had a mound of dishes to get to but we all just
passed on doing anymore than watching another
Lions loss during the annual Thanksgiving game.

December kicked off a very cold month, the winds on the farm were pretty abrasive and often left good sized snow drifts on the north sides of the barns. The horses grew weary being cooped up in the barns, the sheep required additional feed as the grazing was sparse. The girls helped haul feed and often fought through most of the sheep to clean out their pens. Harley made mortal enemies with Thickhead, the ram, that little beast was very territorial and tried to fight anyone that tried to mess with his flock. I often had to rope Thickhead into his own smaller pen to keep him out of trouble so we could get our work done.

Thickhead managed to ram and hit poor Harley in the thigh and it all but knocked her down and her leg left her hobbling for a few days. Jordan was hell bent on dealing with the sheep and stood her ground to fight her way through all of the animals that seemed like a solid wave of wool and bleating heads. Madeline felt sad at each bleat from the lambs as she was worried that she was hurting them, it intimidated her a little bit, Banjo just sat on the side and watched his humans try to do his job.

Harley and Madeline were excited to get to fly home and spend the winter break with their families. Harley looked forward to the break from the hectic snow, even if for only two weeks. Prestly wanted to go home but it wasn't in the budget for her family and she graciously understood. The girls spent adequate time in the gym in the basement, the three took turns on the treadmill while Madeline spent ample down time out in the barn with the horses, of course Harpo had her fair share of whispering in her ear whenever Madeline turned around and startled her causing her to shutter most of the time. Harpo was a silly heart and was a big lover of a horse.

Beck and I tended to as much for the girls as we could, we ensured the girls had the clothes they wanted and Rebecca took them shopping to get their hair done and things of that such. Madeline remained pretty withdrawn and it really bugged me that no one could get her to open up much more. Harley had convinced Prestly to go out for the volleyball team with her so she had an accomplice. I found a writing job that needed a lot of my spare time and I wrote while the girls were in school. I had the girls help to string up Christmas lights to

make the farm more festive, they each fought off
the runny noses and bitter frosty cold as the wind
whipped around.

Rebecca took over most of the chores on her
days off so I could keep up on the new manual that
took most of my time, Banjo laid by my feet when
the house was empty and just chewed on his tennis
ball trying to convince me to play with him. I felt
bad that Banjo was cooped up in the winter, he was
always funny when he would go out, he wound leap
and bound through the higher piles of snow and
bite at any snowball you threw in his direction, he
made it difficult to shovel the walkways.

I took Harley and Madeline to the airport and
made sure that they had what they needed for
their flights home. Rebecca received phone calls
from the Armstrongs and the Navarres when both
of their daughters' arrived home. I hid away in my
study writing and Rebecca spent most of the time
with the girls when they were home for the holiday
break. I gave Rebecca a break to go shopping to
get the girls gifts and I headed out with them so
we could all get things for Rebecca. The holiday
was another nice one and we all exchanged gifts
and watched "The Muppet Christmas carol"; the
greatest holiday movie of all time!!!

It was almost quiet with just Jordan and
Prestly in the house without Harley or Madeline.
Madeline was quiet but she was still another body
in the house. One night Beck and I spoke about how

empty the house will feel when all the girls all went back home at the end of the school year. Rebecca was sad and knew that she was going to miss the ladies but knew that they were just rentals. I wondered how sad Banjo was going to be when all was said and done also.

As the break wound down and school closed in on resuming, Beck offered to go and pick up Madeline and Harley, the girls' flights came in much closer together than they had originally so her afternoon wasn't spent waiting too long. Prestly was looking forward to getting her roommate back but Madeline was only looking forward to getting everything back to as it was.

Beck brought the girls back on a Saturday afternoon and the girls all spent the rest of the night chit chatting and catching up. The missing girls each got the gifts the stay behind girls had gotten for them and the night was capped off watching old black and white "Marx brothers" movies. Banjo was uppity and back to his normal happy self having all of his attention givers back. Beck was glad that all of the girls were safe and back under her watchful eye. We went around the room and asked each girl how they felt about the personal one on one therapy sessions at school compared to the group settings here at the farm. Each girl gave praise for the time Felicia spent with them and felt the group sessions were an accurate team building exercise.

Beck asked if any of the girls had any new thoughts about the issue in the barn and how any of them felt about things. I tensed up at the thought that Jordan and Harley might go back after each other and I was lacking hooks to hang them on to keep them apart. Jordan sat up straighter and told Beck that she didn't have the horror story that the other girls seemed to but she still had plenty of demons to wrestle with when she went back home. Jordan said she enjoyed being at the ranch and the reprieve was greatly appreciated.

Harley said she was reluctant to go back home and risk dealing with her ghosts but seeing her beloved sister Hattie was really missed. Harley apologized to Jordan again for lunging at her in the barn and said that she was just agitated and had a lot on her mind, Prestly piped in and added "we all do." As each girl spoke I contemplated the stories that each girl had told back in the barn, Harley, and Aidens brother Bastian, Prestly and her night on the rock in the park, and poor Madeline. Madeline probably had it the worst in the fact that is was a trusted cousin and she risked seeing her attacker at each family get together.

Prestly explained that being able to speak with Felicia was nice and she liked having someone to confide in, the girls remained fairly superficial in their conversations at first and until the tell all group session, none of the girls had the big picture about one another before the blow out, the girls had different views of each other after. Beck spoke that now the girls were more intimate, not a sexual intimacy but a true emotional intimacy, one that people need in their lives. The girls were each reluctant to share their personal horror stories and kept a hardened shell towards each other; initially.

Once the girls were quasi forced to spill their guts, forced to share, and were also forced to try and trust their stories with one another and as scary as that was, it allowed them to release some of their enormous burden. The girls only had a few weeks after exposing their secrets and they each still seemed guarded after the fact. Beck suggested that the girls work together and trust that each other will keep the secrets and remain trustworthy as confidants.

Beck recommended that the girls try and talk a bit further about their situations with their roommates or with either of us to open up more and possibly get some further perspective from one another, one thing that Rebecca believed was that: if you accept your past and be able to keep it from haunting you over and over, you might be released from the chains it holds you back with. Beck and I each wanted the best for these girls and that their time here gave them each a chance to confront not only their inner demons, but the potential that they could each become and encourage them to do great things. Banjo took to the somber feeling of the room and kept a lower profile so we could each speak.

I suggested each girl contemplate tomorrows group session and Beck and I each reassured them that if they weren't comfortable speaking with us in the group that they could ask us to go away and there would be absolutely no hard feelings whatsoever. We wanted the girls to think of questions or other concerns as the school year was almost half over and in about six months, they would each be heading back home. Each girl felt reluctant but also at ease at the thought of going home, they made their life here work to the best of their ability but it still wasn't their home. I was proud of how well the girls each handled the change of environment and their willingness to adapt.

I told each girl that the change and risk coming here, scared and with no certainty of anything, took courage, going home would take even more. Each girl wished with all of their beings that their histories had never happened, it was unrealistic but completely understandable. Rebecca reminded the girls that she and I were available to question or to vent to if necessary, Harley said she certainly didn't mind kick boxing the punching bag in the gym, Jordan of course ran on the treadmill until exhaustion set in. Madeline sketched in the barn and loved on the horses when Harpo wasn't trying to nuzzle her hair or scare her.

We all sat around and spoke for a while but the inevitable going home was a topic that was silently avoided. I made several plates of my custom nachos, pepper jack cheese and equal amounts of cheddar; nuked to a gooey perfection as we laughed at the eighty year old black and white movies. The night toiled on and we all just settled in and relaxed. Harley was excited to get back to volleyball and Prestly was anxious to try out but lacked the confidence as she was new to the sport.

I was proud of these young girls and the progress they had each made but it was equal to the dread I held in my gut about the long road ahead.

Sunday came and the usual chores were performed, Madeline fed the chickens and filled baskets with eggs while Prestly and Jordan dealt with the sheep, Harley chose to avoid her nemesis Thickhead so she escorted some of the horses out to the Paddocks to get some running done. Felicia was right on time as ten o'clock came . We all made the round of hay bales for benches in the barn so we could sit under the radiant heat lamps. Felicia went around the circle and asked each girl how the break was and questioned Madeline and Harley how they felt when they were at home. All the girls felt safer at the ranch but Felicia explained that mentally they had established a specific perception or view of the ranch and somehow they had to change their views of their own homes also.

The girls were explained that they would have to eventually explain their predicaments and open up to at least their parents, Madeline started to weep at the thought of having to retell her story about her cousin and she was almost paralyzed at the notion of even facing her cousin Charlie. Madeline was shaken and distraught, Jordan sat next to her and gave her a reassuring shoulder bump to suggest that they all had each other for support. I suggested that the girls all swap email addresses and phone numbers all the way around so eventually when they made it back home, they still had their support group. I truly hoped that the girls would be able to fall back on what they learned here and could go with the acquired information that Felicia had shared with them.

Volley ball started and I was tasked with running out after each practice to retrieve Harley and Prestly, I trusted Madeline and Jordan to their own imaginations to hang out on the farm, it was too cold for much trouble as it was anyways. The girls joined me in watching some of the matches and we all cheered on our housemates. The girls performed well and Harley was an aggressive forward and Prestly took to the sport pretty well. The girls practiced volleying back and forth in the living room and it drove Banjo near nuts chasing the ball back and forth trying to get it each time.

The winter dragged on and each girl kept up on their schoolwork and maintained really good grades. The girls worked here and there around the house and continued to learn to cook, they each did their appropriate laundry and further learned simple around the house tasks to better improve themselves in their daily lives. Beck and I shared as much knowledge about life as we could and taught girls what we knew about working with animals and portions of being adults. Madeline did her best to make friends with Lemmy, he was still a jerk but he eased a bit with her when she tried to pet him each time she went to the barn. Madeline was sweet and had a big heart for the massive black horse, maybe she sensed his pain or could relate.

As the spring was coming along I ordered my usual spring solar panels, each spring I added two or three to work with the wind turbines and other panels that lines the roof of the barn to keep working towards having a self sustaining farm. Harley was interested in the electronics and wanted to help with the installation. Jordan kept up with her running to get ready for the upcoming track season at school so she could perform well. Prestly thought about going out for the track team also but wasn't keen on running. Beck and Madeline took out a pair of horses one afternoon to have some time to themselves as Beck was curious if she could pry a bit.

Rebecca wanted to do anything she could to offer some assistance to the smallest girl and try to bond a bit better also. Beck had a lot of concern for Madeline and of the four of them, she probably had the hardest hill to climb. They took out Harpo and Chico to walk the muddy trails through the woods, Madeline loved Harpo, the white pony with gray flecks all over was a goofy horse but also a big lover, she bonded well with her. I got Lemmy used to being saddled but he was still aggressively against being ridden, stupid ass bit at me anytime I motioned getting on him.

The weather began to break and more and more snow melted, the horses enjoyed being out more each day and of course, most of them needed to be hosed off from the mud before being led back into the stalls. Many of the sheep were ready to start dropping lambs in the coming months, I figured I would have better than twenty additions to the herd and in addition to the new babies, I had an increase in required lambs from Sampson as a lot of the local residents ordered lamb from him for Easter meals. I took turns taking the girls with me when I dropped lambs off to the slaughter barn and gave them each a chance to help load and off load sheep each time.

The last Sunday in March was another in depth group therapy session, this time Rebecca decided to encourage each girl to listen as she finally chose to talk about Kaylee. Felicia and I were the only people that knew of all of the details but the girls were oblivious. We initially told the girls that we were tired of hearing about girls all over this country dealing with their own struggles and wanted to help.

Rebecca addressed the group all sitting in a makeshift circle sitting on hay bales listening intently. "Kaylee was twenty-three, she was my younger sister and my best friend" Rebecca started to open up as she fought back tears. "Kaylee had finished her degree in family law and was starting her masters' degree at Wayne State when she had been raped". Kaylee was at a bar with some friends and had met a guy, they seemed to really hit it off that night. The guy she had met had dropped her off at her apartment building after a second date at Mongolian Barbecue. Kaylee texted Rebecca a few times and really liked this guy Kyle.

Kaylee and Kyle seemed very in tune with one another as he was finishing med school and the two of them both had great ambitions for themselves. Rebecca was so proud of her sister and the fruits from her hard work. Kaylee was an intelligent young lady and had her whole future roughly mapped out and she wasn't willing to let a screw up divert her course. Kyle dropped Kaylee off and gave her a sweet gentle kiss on the cheek goodnight and looked very forward to seeing her again.

Kaylee let herself into her apartment building and climbed the stairs to her one bedroom apartment when she was rushed from behind. As she opened her door she was blindsided and shoved into her living room by a much larger man dressed in black. The man kept repeating "*if you scream; you'll die*" as he ripped her close off and violently raped her. Kaylee told Rebecca that the assault lasted over an hour, the man struck Kaylee a few times and ended up fracturing her left cheek bone and detaching her left retina with the large fisted punches.

Kaylee was distraught, she was an emotional wreck after the assault and she had a hard time leaving the couch. After she awoke, after the assault she drove to the hospital and reported the rape, she was frightened but knew that the right thing to do was to report the rape. Detroit had a backlog of rape kits, there is a fund to help better facilitate rape kits and Kaylee often donated funds to help get some of these kits processed to better put some of the criminals behind bars. Kaylee was scared that her attacker might not get caught but a story she read in the Detroit news explained that some of the rapists that were uncovered in the past processed rape kits would have prevented future rapes if the kits would have been processed sooner.

Kaylee hoped with all of her heart that this monster would be locked up and that maybe once that happened, she might be able to get back to her life. Kaylee hid from Kyle despite liking him so much, she was too ashamed of what had happened to take a second date anytime soon, she used a heavy course load as a cover to keep ducking the med student she liked so very much. Kaylee was no longer capable of coping or moving on.

Ch 17

"A month after the rape another troubling situation happened to Kaylee", Rebecca continued to speak about her sister. Kaylee had become really withdrawn and tried her best to keep up on her class loads so her future would remain on track. Kaylee found out that the rape had left her pregnant. It was a horrid situation and it would derail Kaylee completely. Kaylee spoke with Rebecca a few times and cried to uncontrollably when she finally told everything to her older sister. Kaylee was lost and the police had no suspect in the rape.

Kaylee was at a total loss for how to handle everything. Kaylee was absolutely strong in her life until her sense of self was ripped from her, much like the girls that had joined us at our ranch to figure themselves out. Kaylee knew that no matter what she did, her tragedy was now a part of her for the rest of her life. Each girl sat quiet, mouth agape and in shock that this stuff was much more common than just their own situations. The girls kept their eyes locked on my wife whom was telling them of her worst nightmare.

It had been five weeks since the rape and Kaylee had spiraled out of control in her personal life. Kaylee only spoke to Rebecca and was so lost at what to do about it all. Every dark shadowed person that Kaylee passed or saw, caused extreme panick attacks, kaylee couldn't control the shaking horror she felt, each night she didn't feel safe in her own home, she felt physically ill and couldn't sleep at night. Kaylee was losing control and even tried counseling.

After many sleepless nights, no progress from Detroit's "finest" and no way to fix any of the mangled mess that her life had become, Kaylee was left with only one option. Kaylee knew that at the time, her pregnancy was just at a stage that it was just a ball of cells and nothing that even resembled a baby but she knew that even if she aborted the forced conception, she would still be burdened with the assault. Kaylee was lost, scared, tormented with the actions of some animal. Rebecca was scared for her sister, terrified about everything that had happened and felt lost that she couldn't do anything to help.

Kaylee knew that many people failed when they tried to commit suicide and it left them in different stages of disabled or what have you. Kaylee thought up backup plans if her first route of suicide didn't work so no matter what, she wouldn't wake up. Kaylee wrote a long and very detailed letter to her parents and deeply apologized that she had no other options, She had written letters to her sister Rebecca and her parents so they had a last, thoughtful hand written "thank you and I love you" from her and that October night was her last.

The email sent to Rebecca and her parents led them to contact the police, Rebecca drove to Detroit while I was out on a business trip, I was stricken with grief that my wife had to join the police without me and enter Kaylee's apartment. Rebecca had to identify her sister, lifeless and in the tub. Beck had to place the phone call to her parents and break the awful news. Rebecca was hardly able to drive back to the ranch that night. I flew home early after Rebecca had called and told me what happened. My wife was inconsolable and it took everything I had in me to get her out of bed, even for the funeral.

Rebecca took a few months off of work and sank deeply into depression, as well as our bed. I insisted Rebecca seek counseling to talk about everything she had to work out about the loss of her beloved sister. It took me two months to get Rebecca out of bed, I waited on her hand and foot, fed her in bed, bathed her and did my best to take care of her, even after the months, I still can't paint finger nails to save my life. After the two month of having fingers painted as if by someone with cerebral palsy, Beck finally decided to shower herself and give therapy a try.

Being a nurse, she knew that depression was terrible and she wanted to get back to helping others, she had to find a way to stop crying long enough to do it. After a month of therapy, Rebecca tried going back to work, she started off on half shifts once or twice a week to get her reacquainted with being out of the house. At the time we only had a dozen or so sheep and two horses to tend to so I decided that my wife needed some additional love, and someone to need her attention to distract her a bit. Once some of the weather got better and Rebecca was back to working full time, I drove out early one day right after Beck had headed out to work, I came back with a small fuzzy spotted ball of energy, this is when Banjo came to be.

Banjo was wound to the max with energy, this four-legged crime scene was into everything he could reach. The first day alone he chewed into his big bag of food, causing a mountain of puppy chow to spill across the kitchen floor, which then he chased each moving pellet and rolled in the rest. Over the first month of his presence, Banjo chewed any and all elastic he could find, we had piles of underwear ruined, he chewed the underwire out of a dozen bras, and played tug of war with all of the house plants, then ate the dirt from them, he was the devil.

After a month or two of running the little beast, he calmed down a tad, Rebecca and I each had to keep a close eye on him to curtail his deviant urges, we trained him with verbal and hand commands, we worked him with the sheep and he took on his jobs better each day. Rebecca slowly broke the depression and got back to herself and we got back to being us over the following months. Beck explained to the girls that it took a while to get over all of the hurt and she continued to see her shrink for the following year or so. The girls asked a few questions of my wife and they all revolved around the letters and the mentality of Kaylee when she took her life. Beck could only describe her as "terrified" Kaylee tried to get some help but wasn't open enough to be willing to let herself be helped and that was a big part of it all.

Rebecca wanted to disappear into her bed and never see the light of day again when she first got the news. Beck couldn't imagine one day being *OK* with everything that had happened, people told her that time heals all wounds, it doesn't in fact, everything seems just as real and present and that it still hurt. Scars do heal, they don't go away but they serve as reminders that what tried to stop you; but failed. I showed the scar that Beck got to stitch on my arm, Harley finally removed her black sleeve and showed off all of the self inflicted scars on her left arm. We all knew about Harley's fingers but she said that each time she had to wrangle a glove over her paralyzed fingers that she wished she had never done what she did. "Suicide doesn't stop the pain, it stops the chance for things to get better."

Beck hung her head and wept as she missed her sister all over again. The girls started to speak among themselves and discuss that none of them wanted to be victims any longer. Madeline spoke up and expressed her deep looming fear of reprisal in her family if she broke her silence, Harley explained that if she spoke up about her attack that she would not only be letting her parents Jill and Paul down, that she would have to face the entire school that was already against her. I told the girls that they had support here, one another to rely on and that being totally honest and vulnerable to the people around them, that they were allowing themselves to trust enough to be open for help.

I was proud of the steps that the girls had taken and I mentioned to each of them that they should walk taller in their progress. Felicia told each of them that as young adults that they would each have to make future decisions for themselves, regardless if it was for college or for a future spouse. The girls giggled at the mention of a potential spouse and I forbode boys for the time being and trusting boys was a soft spot among most of them. Harley put her sleeve back on, not only to hide her scars from the others, but probably to also hide them from herself.

The runny noses signified that our time in the barn was probably surpassing the allotted time and that we should finish up some of the chores and get the hay spread into the stalls. Felicia let the girls know that she would be willing to come out for support at any time if any of the girls wanted to conference call their parents to divulge any of their secrets. None of the girls expressed that desire and Jordans' mom already knew her troubles. Jordan took to staying late after school and spending her spare time in the public library near the school while Harley and Prestly were in volleyball.

It was quiet with Madeline and I at the ranch, just us and Banjo. I hung around the stalls with Madeline as she sketched and I cleaned many of the cobwebs out from the heater grates and tops of the stall walls. I watched Madeline softly convince the irate pitch black horse Lemmy to come to her and let her pet him, she had a way of soothing the monster and he actually let her pet him quite a bit. I was actually jealous of the petite girl and tried to take mental notes of her advances to him.

I had the idea to have Madeline sooth his wild side as I saddled him with a blanket and saddle; he actually remained at ease with her comforting him. I was thoroughly impressed at her softness and her ability to keep him calm. Madeline and I brushed the stallion together and I felt like I made more progress in that afternoon than in the whole previous year he had been at the ranch.

CH 18

I took the opportunity of the one on one time with Madeline to try to get her to open up a bit more. I told her that I felt bad about what Charlie did to her, it was senseless and mean. I tried to educate her on the inner mind of a juvenile boy and that they never think of the next step for anything. I tried to set her at some sort of ease that I suspected that he wasn't out to ruin her life, even if that's what he did, but that he was just brainless and weak to his urges. Madeline took a big step to the side and gave me a dreadful look, half a second later I realized why she took the step away and I had to jump back to defend my actions, Madeline smiled a bit and had a slight giggle to her as she explained that she was just joking.

I was impressed that she was finally opening up a bit and felt comfortable enough to joke and bust my chops. I congratulated her on her making me uncomfortable and reassured her that no one but my wife had my interest. Madeline told me that she was tired of hurting, sick of being scared and hated her cousin for each inappropriate touch and how he made her feel. Madeline spoke about how she didn't know what was going on as he touched her, made her touch him and as she grew older, she felt worse and worse as she learned more about the "birds and the bees." I felt sick right along side her, knowing what this poor girl had been through.

Madeline asked how she was supposed to get through everything, all I could come up with was "one day at a time" I felt like a cliche and a let down, I wished I could offer more advice to this struggling young lady but the truth was, I just couldn't. I suggested that she speak more, give others' a chance to get to know her, not for their sake but for hers, to let herself be herself, to find the strength and courage to face the world. Madeline felt like she couldn't trust her parents, they left her in the care of her cousin and victim to his ways. She knew they couldn't have known what was going on but she still blamed them a little.

I told her that Beck had blamed herself for the choice Kaylee made to take her own life, it was ultimately Kaylee's decision and it had nothing to do with Rebecca but Rebecca still felt like there should have been more that she could have done. I explained to Madeline how much my heart ached with overwhelming desire to help my wife, almost as much as she wished she could have helped her sister. I told Madeline that even though I didn't have kids of my own, I sensed that all parents, or at least the good ones, wanted nothing but the best for their kids and should be willing to do anything for them.

The news is stricken with murdering criminals and scum of the earth but yet, many of the parents still stuck by their children even when they committed atrocities. I told Madeline to think about telling her mother the painful truth. Madeline shied away a bit when I made my suggestion but I told her that even after she went home, she was always welcome to call and talk to either Beck or I or even if things were too tough, that she could opt to come back again anytime she and her parents felt necessary.

Madeline thanked me graciously for opening our home to offer the opportunity to the girls and give them a retreat from their lives and come and get a clean slate. I told her that it was all my wifes dream and that she did most of the work to make everything happen. We finished up brushing Lemmy with his saddle on so he would get better used to being saddled again, he was a race horse in his previous life and anytime you put a saddle on him he was ready to run. Madeline and I geared up and headed into to town to pick up the other girls. Madeline told me that each of the other girls were equally appreciative for what Beck and I offered to them and they spoke about how great the farm was when they were alone.

Madeline sat fairly quietly in the passenger seat as Banjo sat on her lap, he wasn't about to let someone steal his spot. I reminded Madeline that this town was simply temporary strangers and she could be anyone she wanted to be, and that in a few months, she would be gone and never see any of them again if she didn't want to. Family were just strangers you felt obligated to loan money to, even if they didn't deserve it. She raised a quizzical eyebrow, I told her to not just look at them as people she was obligated to love and support and whatever else, she had the strength to pick and chose who she would allow into her life, family or not.

Madeline liked the idea of choosing her own family, she could include these girls if she wanted to, she could also exclude Charlie or any others she possibly simply shared blood with. I told her that life was just memories, many of which hadn't happened yet and she had a lot more control over the memories yet to come. If she wanted a memory of Ireland, "then dang it girl go get that memory," that cost me another raised eyebrow, with a side of an awkward chuckle. I felt like a bit of a dork and I am certainly aware that I'm not some cheesy teen but she got the hint at what I was trying say. As we pulled into the school parking lot we could see Jordan jogging back from the library and she got to the walk way as we parked the truck.

The three of us wandered through the hallway heading towards the gym to let Harley and Prestly know that we were there to pick them up. The girls were doing cool down stretches and Harley pointed at their school gear, Madeline and Jordan picked up the backpacks to help and we all headed out to the truck, Banjo right behind us. Harley and Prestly complained about being sweaty and smelly, I completely agreed with them but didn't want to sucker punch their confidence. Banjo kept hitting the door lock the entire drive home, he was driving me nuts as the locks kept fidgeting up and down every time he hit the button, Jordan kept him in her lap on the passenger side and kept cracking the window to grasp for some fresh air in the truck.

Madeline and Jordan helped to prepare dinner while the other two quick showered to be less offensive. We laid out plenty of veggies for dinner, the girls laughed in unison as a cherry tomato hit the floor, Banjo tried to eat it but kept letting it fall out of his mouth as he didn't like tomatoes, he just wouldn't let it go, he kept trying to eat it but he just couldn't force himself to swallow it. I finally was able to stop laughing hard enough to take it from him and get us all back to dinner. Beck was running late coming home from work so I made her a plate to eat later when she was able to join us.

After dinner, the girls finished homework, Jordan got hers done at the library as well as some additional research for her own benefit. Madeline sat with Prestly and Harley as they did their work, she was able to provide very good insight when it came to algebra. Madeline was really good at math and she was embracing a more outgoing personality. The girls welcomed the more talkative girl and complimented her on her choice to open up. I asked Jordan what she had been up to with all of this time at the library and if she was having any luck.

Jordan had pulled a fast one, she was organizing things to apply for a small business loan. She had an idea to start a health food store that was also full of running gear. Jordan said she found a few government grants that were available to minorites. Jordan spoke to her mom to see how she felt about moving out of Gilbert and maybe to the other side of Tuscon or Phoenix maybe. Corina was excited at the idea that Jordan had had and was willing to do anything she could to help.

Jordan had many of her assets covered, she located a building that had three apartments on the second floor and Jordan was already in contact with all parties necessary to get things going as soon as she moved back. With Corina and one other renter, Jordan could work for free in her own store for the summer until things took off a bit, she hoped that her mother could work for her while she was in school once the school year resumed back in Arizona. I was really surprised that Jordan had the ambition to propagate all of this herself and she had covered so many of her contingents diligently.

Corina was picking up extra shifts and saving every extra penny she could get, she wanted to be able to help her daughter start this business as well as one day stop working for other people in two jobs. I offered any resources I had including the internet for contact etcetera if she needed it. Jordan wanted to stay hush hush on her venture so it wouldn't be such a let down if things fell through; it made sense to me. I was quickly recruited to hoping that things worked out for Jordan, I was seriously impressed at how thorough she was and how detailed her business plan was evolving. I kept Jordans secret for her sake, except for my wife of course.

I suggested to Jordan that she share with her housemates but she said she would, in time. Prestly woke up sick one morning in mid-April, she was violently ill and had to miss the day of school. I let her stay and flip channels on the couch with a glass of Sierra Mist and a bucket to keep her company if she were to need it. I made my rounds through the barn, Banjo rode along as we checked all of the fences and wires, I had heard a few coyotes in the previous night so I wanted to make sure that my animals were safe. I kept tabs on Prestly as I worked in my day, she was miserable to say the least but I suspected it was something like food poisoning and not flu related hopefully, I was

deeply hopeful that I wasn't about to have a house
full of sick young girls, nurse wife or not.

April was getting warmer, I was making more frequent runs to Sampsons' to drop off lambs three and four at a time, he was helping me thin my herd as the baby lambs were starting to drop out. I had about forty-five to fifty sheep, and with better than twenty babies on the way, I was about to have wool up to my ears. The girls were giddy about the baby lambs and they all wanted to chase the little critters about and hold them forever. Banjo chased the crows away that were picking at the piles of placenta littering the fields. The girls helped me to spot and keep an eye out in the field for the new mothers and their babies.

We separated the new mother sheep from the herd and penned them with their babies so they would be left alone from Thickhead and any other larger sheep that pushed and risked trampling the unsteady lambs, as well as give plenty of nursing time. After a few weeks the baby lambs would be given their shots and tagged with yellow ear tags for identification. The girls ran about among the tiny lambs, they just couldn't get enough of the soft critters. Volleyball was coming to a close and I was glad to save some of the additional trips to and from the school.

Easter Sunday was another pleasant meal with plenty of friends. Randy made it, Mike and Annie, Sampson and Winston and of course, Felicia, my farm became an unofficial work retreat for Mike, Annie and Felicia, and they all joked about it accordingly. The girls were a tad nervous after having seen the three adults around the school more as authority figures than just friends of mine and Becks' like they initially did. The girls ate their fill and helped to clear the table and worked to help clean up after all was said and done.

Jordan asked if they could go for a horse ride after things cleared out and Rebecca and I saddled up Zeppo, Harpo, Chico and Groucho. The girls rode for over an hour after the mid-day meal while the other adults just kicked back and spoke about the upcoming summer. Randy was intrigued to help install the solar panels as he had the previous two years and was curious as to how well I was making out with all of the green adjacent power supplies, the wind turbines and solar panels.

Mike wasn't totally convinced he was up for cutting hay until Randy jumped in that he "only drove the tractor." Annie commented that she was looking forward to several nights sitting out on the patio sipping cocktails with Beck and Felicia, Felicia agreed. I was trying to keep a watchful eye towards the woods and I was able to semi watch the horses trace back and forth in the woods, I trusted the girls to ride but was also mildly nervous because the girls were still petite and the horses could be a task once in a while. Felicia totally busted me concerning for the girls and the horses and exposed my concern, she also reassured me that she had been riding with the girls many times during their group sessions and also semi taught them how to ride. Felicia encouraged me to trust them and stop sweating things.

I snapped too and tried to rejoin the adults in conversation but out of the corner of my eye, I kept trying to look out for the girls. Felicia said that the girls were doing well at school but left everything else confident between her and her subjects, Annie said she could back Felicia up and that the girls' grades were excellent and not once has any of their names graced across her desk in the office. Winston just stared off at the chickens as his attention wasn't required for the dominate conversation. Randy and Sampson spoke about the market and upcoming potential work. Sampson had the parking lot paved not that long ago and added plenty of parking but was thinking about upgrading the lighting for his later hours.

Randy suggested high intensity lights, similar to those used in stadiums.

Randy and Sampson discussed the Market and poor Winston looked as bored as he could possibly be. I offered Winston a break from the school or market talk and we headed into the garage. I showed off buckshot and the progress I was slowly making while I had off time from everything. I was close to finishing everything else except rebuilding the engine. Winston offered to help me with the engine, he spent some time working a few summers at a mechanic shop so he could offer some advice as to fine tune the motor to put out a few extra horsepower.

Winston explained that he could up the power with some higher compression pistons and not even have to bore out the engine. I was intrigued to see what the young man had to offer and also offered to pay him for his time. I knew that even though he was taking online classes to make the most efficient use of his time, I also knew that he was off to college in the fall to better cement himself a much brighter future than he might have had back in Ypsi. Winston was a very bright young man and he was very honorable, he was a great sidekick for Sampson and I knew Sampson was going to miss his compadre that he had trained and taught over the last two or three years.

Winston had my respect as he treated everyone fairly. He learned a lot business and persona from Sampson and took on that cool air that Sampson seemed to breathe. We poked around the garage for a bit before hearing the girls come riding back up to the barn. I headed through the door to help the girls stall the horses, Winston wasn't a fan of such large animals so he hightailed it back up to the patio. The girls were light and giggly and laden with bright red noses from the cooler air. They seemed to really get along finally and they enjoyed the ride on their own. The girls stabled the horses and then put away all of the tackle that the girls used on each horse.

Banjo couldn't decide which group of people he could get the most attention from so he bounded back and forth between the patio and the gaggle of girls in the barn. The girls had stepped up their riding a bit and rather than mosey along they trotted with a bit more gusto to exercise the horses and give themselves a freeing mild run on the soupy trails, they had a great time from the way things sounded. I was relieved that the girls had been able to breathe easier and relax on the farm.

The holiday was coming to a close and everyone finished their chores before the light slipped away into the horizon. I sat with my beautiful wife in the living room as the girls hustled and bustled around upstairs preparing for bed. One by one the girls yelled goodnight and we responded in kind. Banjo sat in the middle of the chaos upstairs but came lumbering back down to sit with us as we watched some old episodes of "Scrubs" to finish off our fun filled day. I was totally exhausted but the quiet time with Rebecca was long overdue.

It was mid-April and the end of the school year closed in, I asked Rebecca how she felt about everything we had gone through. She felt much more closure when it came to her situation regarding Kaylee, she would forever miss her younger sister but felt that by extending her heart and help to the girls upstairs; that she was keeping her sisters' memory alive. Rebecca and I had grown a lot over the last several months, it feels like we had come a great distance. I was completely exhausted, not just physically but emotionally as I tried to keep a balance on the farm and all of the girls that were under my care.

I was still worried about Madeline more so than any of the others. She was still troubled, despite finally coming out of her shell better, she was still closed off a bit. I pondered Jordans' business hopes and I hoped things turned out for her and her mother Corina. There was a small part of me that found comedy in the tenacious Dr. Cox in the TV series and thought that maybe I could pull off the gruff caretaker like persona but I didn't have dozens of writers to script my rants and changing my attitude towards the girls might make them uncomfortable. My eyelids grew heavy,

I was fading quickly but I didn't want the night to end, once the morning came, the chores and rushing around madness with the girls was soon to follow. Rebecca and I retired to bed and the day finally came to an end.

The alarm screeched loudly; and wearily I arose. Beck was close behind me in our morning routine of rubbing our eyes and trying to shake off the sleepy residue. I heard some rustling down the hall, which meant at least one of the other girls were awake. I dressed in my work clothes and headed down the stairs to start the teapot. Rebecca got the girls moving as I prepared her and I our Irish breakfast tea to accompany our morning. I offered each girl hot chocolate to pep start but each denied the offer to forgo the calories, the morning wasn't as cold as so many of the others anyways. Madeline remained quiet, Jordan had enough spunk to compensate for the silence.

Harley and Prestly weren't the most cheerful in the morning and they half dragged their feet in accordance with their moods but we all headed out to the barns. I got to work moving horses with Prestly while Madeline and Jordan started to shovel stalls, the roommates worked together pretty well. Harley climbed up into the loft to start dropping fresh hay bales down to refill the stalls with. Once all of the horses were outside I got to mixing feed buckets, Prestly took Banjo out to the sheep barn and gave him commands to move the herd to the second pasture before they had to head back in and freshen up for the school day.

The girls stayed on task pretty well and the youth must have been their secret to being able to get up early, bust their butts and still have the energy to keep going all day. I was glad to lay low for a bit during the days once the girls were off to school, frankly, I was tired of all of the craziness. Rebecca was off for the day and she sketched out her new garden ideas while I snuck a bit of a nap. Banjo slumped to sleep on my legs while we laid out on the couch for an hour or so. Beck woke me up and suggested I turn the garden over while she cleaned up the landscaped portions of the yard.

The weather was growing warmer and we were all gracious for the improvement. I loved watching my wife get down and dirty, she loved to work with her hands and I didn't mind feasting on the fruits of my labor later in the summer. Rebecca was alive with the new garden ideas and we both loved to toil around the yard. Banjo would always end up digging in the freshly turned dirt of the garden and it took a while to wash to brat when he was covered head to nubbed tail with dirt. The upside to Banjo, he wasn't afraid of a bath and he almost seemed to get dirty on purpose just so Rebecca and I had to bathe him, with as smart as he is, the deviance wouldn't surprise me the least.

CH 20

The girls offloaded from the bus, Jordan and Madeline made it home while Harley and Prestly were finishing their volleyball season. The girls spoke about their days, Madeline was taking to her freshman year well but she was still shy and guarded. I hoped that in time Madeline would find the confidence in herself to open up and start to let more people in, not to spill her secrets but to honestly start to trust people better.

The volleyball season wrapped up and they ended their season with an honorable record. Felicia was a strong coach and she made the girls work together admirably. Felicia kept up with her individual sessions during the school week and the group sessions on Sundays when she came over to work with Elvis. The girls grew stronger in their bonds as housemates but also as young women. We celebrated the birthdays that came and went and each girl kept in close contact with their families back home several times per week. The Armstrongs were anxious to get Madeline back, the Navarres to get Harley back and Prestly was ready to go home.

Jordan was ready to start the more adult portion of her life. Jordan had been filling out paperwork to apply for grants for both her and her mother Corina, Corina checked out buildings to house the business venture she and her daughter had been working towards, she found a local realestate agent to guide her through walk-ins and show her around and she would speak to Jordan about her findings. I contacted a realestate friend of mine, Vance Shutes to work with Jordan and help explain some of the odds and ends of the jargon.

Jordan was approved a good sized grant from the government for minority business owners and she was ready to start ordering supplies to fill her shop with once she was back home. Corina found an awesome location for her business in Tuscon, Corina wasn't a big fan to upheave her whole apartment and move by herself but she was excited to give her daughter a solid start to her future. Jordan had spent many hours after her homework was done designing a layout and how her storefront would look. Jordan's excitement was overwhelming and some nights she would go for extra long runs with Banjo to tire out her excitement.

Things were progressing quickly as the school year was coming to a close. Baby lambs were coming from all over it seemed, I made the weekly sheep deliveries to Sampson and as the month turned to May, things got more busy around the farm. I was cooking out a few times a week, Randy was always there for grilled foods of any sorts, Shutes came out one night to facilitate lease signing attributes for Jordans new building to start as of June first and the other girls were keeping busy also. Things were teeming with the nice weather and the animals were more uppity. Banjo kept to his mischievous rubbing against the chicken pens and growling at the birds on the other side of the thin wire.

Jordan was ever busy with her upcoming business, Harley was still kickboxing with the punching bag in the basement and Prestly was doting on the the little lambs in the barns every chance she got. Meanwhile Madeline was always to be found in the barn, doodling and sketching the horses, Beck and I tried to keep up with each girl and make sure that they each girl had our individual attention and ample opportunities to unburden themselves onto us if the need arose. Mike and Annie joined Felicia and the crew on a Sunday after noon in the first weekend in May, we grilled more than enough veggies and chicken and ate like kings. The weather in the distance looked like we were in for a wallop, the weather was warm but the breeze smelled like a torrential downpour in the forecast.

The horses paced in their paddocks and that was usually a sign of rough weather headed our way. I had the girls stable the horses while Prestly and Rebecca used Banjo to barn the sheep. The weather darkened and the sky began to turn a dark green. The nasty wicked weather was rolling in with an angry force and the visitors left to get home safely. I was certain the storm at hand was going to make a mess of things so the group all headed inside to put a movie in and just wait for it to pass.

The thunder started to bellow and the lightning crack as the hours grew late. The rain began to pound at the barn and it rattled the windows as it fell. The temperature in the house fell and the girls each ducked into hooded sweatshirts. Banjo was wrought with nervous energy and jumped at each thunderous boom. Prestly stroked Banjo to keep him calm and Madeline kept a weary eye out the window to watch the lightning brighten up the sky. I kicked my feet up as I sat with my wife and we just turned up the volume on the movie to drown out the noise right outside. I tried my best to corral my thoughts from wandering outside to my animals and reassured myself that animals have that sense to keep calm during nasty weather.

There was a loud boom outside and a few seconds later, the power zapped out. The weather grew darker and now the house matched it. Beck and I calmed the girls down as we stumbled around

to light candles I had a few power packs to plug
cell phones into, I turned on the battery powered
radio to some oldies and kept a weary ear out for
emergency broadcast warning just in case we
needed to head to the basement to avoid a
potential tornado. The girls calmed down when we
had plenty of candles lit to illuminate the house.

Suddenly the phone rang, there weren't
many people that had the house phone number, it
was used mostly to find a misplaced cell phone that
often found its' way into a couch cushion or that
Banjo had chased across a floor and under the
couch. I answered the phone to hear the old
farmer from down the road on the other end.
Ronnie Wilson had a problem, he had a tree branch
knock down a fence and he had a few cows get out
of their field. I was unsure how I was about to help,
I needed the girls hands but the weather sucked
and I didn't want to be out in it, especially with
the lightning.

I told my crew about the phonecall and Beck
was ready to help. The girls all agreed that
something needed to be done and each were willing
to saddle up and help. Each of us grabbed a poncho
and a headlight to brighten our way. We scurried
out to the barn and each began the task of
mounting up horses. Beck readied Groucho,
Madeline Harpo, Prestly calmed Chico, Jordan
mounted up on Elvis, Harley was nervous about her
first time on Zeppo and even though I was scared
out of my mind, I sized up Lemmy.

Lemmy was oddly calm when I mounted him for the first time and I spoke to him and told him what we needed to do. Beck and I each grabbed some rope for a lassos, not something either of us were good at or even practiced much but we were sure it would come in handy. Beck opened the side door before mounting Grouch and after the girls were safely on their horses. I told the girls to stay tight and keep up with Beck and I. I wasn't sure how the horses would take to the storm and I was really freaked out about Lemmy, I hoped with all of myself that this bonehead wouldn't do anything stupid and freak out.

We headed down the driveway and out the front gate, it was hard to see and we kept trying to keep our lamps on the road in front of us. Lemmy handled being ridden pretty well but I had to keep a tight hold on the reigns to keep him from bolting too far ahead. I yelled to the girls that we had to ride about a mile down the road before we got to the neighboring farm, the horses would be a great hand but I really worried about the girls. I've fallen off of horses and sure it stings, I'm also twice the age of the girls and if anyone might get hurt, I'd prefer it to be me. We kept a fast pace while we headed to Wilsons, the farmer was outside with his rain slicks and flashlights as we got near the farm.

We circled the farmer than needed our help and he explained that probably five or six cows got out on the far side of the farm. Wilson offered to stand near the fence opening to keep the cows in and let in the ones that got out. I was nervous to task each girl with gathering a cow but informed them that if they rode by the cow they could lead the stray beasts back to the fence where Ronnie stood by. We headed to the far field and searched down the wayward cows, I had Prestly and Harley close on my side as Beck headed further down with the other girls. I didn't like my wife not being by my side but I knew the girls had the necessary riding skills and that they would step up and perform. It was raining hard and the lightning made it fairly simple to spot the cows in the field when everything lit up brightly.

I could see the lights of the far pack of girls when I wiped the rain out of my eyes. My jeans were soaked and Lemmy felt tense under my legs but I kept telling him he was being a good boy. Prestly got near one of the cows and yelled at her to head back to the farm, Prestly broke off to steer the cow back to Ronnie at the fence break. Harley and I located another cow and maneuvered around to get the cow turned back to the farm next. I could see a light in the distance but I couldn't hear much beyond the rain hitting my poncho and the horses sloshing in the mud. With another crack of lightning I could see another cow in the distance speeding farther away from the farm,

I yelled to Harley that this cow was hers and I turned Lemmy towards the distancing cow.

Harley responded that she had it and that I was on my own. My heart raced and pounded as hard as the rain did as I gave the heel kick to Lemmy that this was his time to shine. Lemmy didn't take more than a second to get his clue and he was off. Lemmy sped faster than the lightning that cracked over head, his bulging shoulders rubbed against my inner thighs against the saddle and his stride was intense. Lemmy had amazing speed and he splashed through the puddling mud in the field. The rain stung my eyes as we flew through the field toward our target cow. Lemmy seemed to feel free as he ran.

We neared the running cow and I pulled tighter on the reigns to slow him gown. I calmed Lemmy by talking to him and "whoaing" him to ease his running pace. Lemmy whipped his head around slinging his wet mane around and he seemed playful as he did it. I could feel a relief in his muscles from atop the slick black beast, I felt that I had finally bonded with the boy after the long year plus that he'd been at the farm and we'd spent trying to size up one another.

I roped the stray cow and tugged along to convince it to stay by my side. I looped the rope around the saddle horn so I didn't get pulled off of Lemmy. I found confidence in the stallion and wondered if maybe he needed to be let loose and run more often, maybe that would ease him up and make him more friendly. The cow tugged with resistance and I could feel Lemmy pull back under the saddle. I could count five light spots over near the fence as Lemmy and I trotted back. I petted and thanked my horse for his spectacular performance in the wet weather.

I was proud of Lemmy, all of the bodies from my ranch stepped up in a big way. In the country we all did what we could to help one another and I was glad to offer our help to Ronnie. Ronnie was an older gentleman and made his livelihood with the stubborn cows of his farm. I got closer to the gap that Ronnie stood guard at. Everyone made it back from what I could tell after frequently clearing rain from my eyes.

As I got closer I realized something was wrong, there was a headlamp on the ground and everyone was standing around in the mud. I lead the cow into the pasture and hopped off Lemmy with a calming pat to his pulsing neck. I walked Lemmy to Beck and shouted my questions to what was going on. Zeppo was tied to the fence and Harley was on the ground screaming. Zeppo handled what she needed to but when nearing the fence, the cow kicked and Zeppo bucked Harley off. Harley was holding her leg as she writhed in pain. The other girls were worried and beginning to panick.

I shouted that they all needed to calm down. I ordered Jordan to lead Prestly and Madeline back to the farm, they needed to undo the horses and get back into the farm house. The weather was not letting up, the rain poured down on all of us and we still had work to do. Beck tied up Groucho to the fence and helped Wilson to half rig the fence to keep the cows in through the rest of the night. Beck and Wilson worked feverishly to get their work done before the lightning struck closer and closer with each menacing bolt. The horses tugged at the fence and the stomped at the mud nervously.

I checked where Harley was hurting, she was grabbing her leg and pelvis and she cried out as she described the pain near her groin. I was worried about Harley and asked if she could manage riding back to the farm, she hesitantly agreed that she could because she would have to, everything was so loud with the rain and the storm. I made sure Beck was good when she was done and with her help to steady Zeppo, I heaved Harley back onto her saddle. Harley couldn't get her foot into her stirrup so I shoved it in and calmed Lemmy before getting back onto him. Beck mounted back onto Groucho and the three of us headed back down the road to the farm. Harley cried and grunted with each trot Zeppo took. I felt horrible for the girl, she was tough but this had to have been something major.

We got back to the farm, I unloaded Harley onto the screened porch and laid her down so I could call one of the other girls to help Beck put the horses away. Madeline was right inside the door and was still in her soaking wet clothes, ready to help. Madeline was dearly worried about Harley and wanted to know what was going on, you could see the dread on her face. I yelled to Beck that I was taking Harley to the hospital and that she was up to the rest. I loaded the soaking wet girl, covered in mud, into the passenger side of my truck, Jordan ran me my cell phone so I could stay in touch and we were off.

The drive to the hospital took better than forty-five minutes and in the weather, pushed us back more than an hour. Harley screamed and cried as I tried to drive carefully to the ER. Harley thanked me for taking care of her but also grunted and clenched her teeth trying to be tough. I sped into the ER and my tires screeched on the wet pavement. I hustled around the front of the truck to find a wheelchair and offloaded my passenger. Harley tried to hang onto my neck as I scooped her up and moved her out of the truck.

The ER was busy with people, I was surprised at the personnel that were rummaging about. I filled out the necessary paperwork while Harley fought the pain as best she could. I sent a text to Rebecca that we were in and waiting for triage. Beck responded that Lemmy kicked Madeline but other than a nasty bruise and small gash on her shin, she would be fine. I felt like things were falling apart, I had two hurt girls and I was responsible for both of them. My head pounded and I was distraught at everything that had transpired.

The wait to be seen seemed to be the longest hour I had ever experienced in my life. Harley was starting to dry and the mud that caked her back half was started to crust and fall all over the floor. Harley was yawning a lot and getting tired as her adrenaline was wearing out. I too was growing tired and could go for a Diet Pepsi for a pick me up. I offered Harley anything she wanted from the vending machine but she declined. I grabbed a cold 20 ounce bottle and made it back to her side just as her name was called out.

I hopped up and wheeled the young lady back into the triage room, she was barraged with questions. I offered to step out if she needed the privacy regarding any of the awkward personal questions. Harley didn't care, she answered the necessary girly based questions like a pro, without hesitation and then we went back to an emergency room. The room was small, surrounded with a white curtain and a stretcher bed in the middle. The nurse told her that she would have to get out of her wet clothes and into a hospital gown. Harley nodded that she understood and told me that I'd be the one doing the task. I knew what I had to do and I'm sure it felt equally uneasy for the two of us for what I was about to have to do.

I laid the gown across her torso and helped her out of her soaking wet hoodie. I warned Harley that it was time to get a little more personal and to bear with me as I had to work off her tight wet pants. Harley apologized that her undies weren't coordinated then chuckled a bit. I smirked off her remark and dropped her hoodie on her lap to keep some dignity about the matter. I unbuttoned her pants and began to work them off of her as she kept a tight grasp on her leg. She cried out at the pain that was caused by the wet pants pulling at her hurt leg. Her left thigh had a nasty bruise starting already and she grabbed at her leg to hold it.

I sat Harley up a bit to put a second gown on, Harley was glad to be mostly dry and I piled up her clothes on the top of the cart that sat in the room. Harley told me that Zeppo bucked when they got near the fence and thunder clapped spooking her horse. She said she half landed on her left leg and that's when she felt a massive agonizing pain in her leg when she hit the ground. I suggested to Harley that she lay back and relax I told her how proud I was that she took charge like a boss and performed what she was suppose to do. She handled Zeppo and the cow very well and that she did it all just as good as the adults, if not better. I told Harley that we should be out soon enough and that I'd get her back to bed as soon as I could; it was getting late.

A doctor came in and took notes about everything that happened, I was asked to step out as he had a few additional questions. I walked down the hall closer to the outside wall to send Rebecca a text, a text from her came in and she let me know that she was able to glue the gash in Madelines shin and get everyone calmed down and into bed. Beck said she would be on the couch waiting for us to return and to just hang in there. I sent her a text that the doc was just now seeing her and asking questions and I had no idea how much longer we would be.

I noticed the doctor walk back out and I headed to her direction to get an update. She informed me that she gave Harley some pain meds and that she was ordering some x-rays. I had the same suspicion as the doctor, we both were thinking it was a broken leg, I felt terrible. I slid back in past the curtain keeping Harley separated from the outside hallway, I asked her how she was feeling, her response was less than lady like but appropriate for her situation. I encouraged her to relax and think about anything but her leg.

Some people came in to get her for her x-rays, they wheeled her whole bed out rather than move her about with her leg hurting so bad, I kicked my feet out as I sat in the chair and waited for her return. Harley came back smiling and slurring after her exam, apparently her pain meds had kicked in while they snapped the few pictures of her thigh. Harley was giggly and relaxed as her pain had chemically subsided. Harley was funny and it was almost a complete personality change when she let her rigid guard down and didn't have her normal chip on her shoulder, she closely mimicked a young happy teen girl.

After a while of letting Harley rest and me nervously pacing in the small confines of the emergency room, the doc came back in and let us know the latest update about her leg, sure enough it had a spiral fracture from falling on it, the good news was that it was only fractured and hadn't actually broke, but nonetheless, Harley was going to be fixed with a cast on her leg for the next month or so. Harley was upset that she would be stuck sitting around for her last month on the farm but her bummed state was overshadowed by her meds keeping her giggly and smiley.

After tons of discharge papers and loading up my exhausted little farmhand, we were on our way back to the ranch. Harley was freezing in the flimsy hospital gowns but her clothes were still wet and muddy. I kept the heat up even though I was sweating like crazy, I could smell myself sweating barbecue sauce. Harley laid back in the seat and slept most of the slow way home, I still felt terrible that she broke her leg but was also relieved that she was going to be OK. I pulled back into the driveway and I could see the candles flicker in the house through the windows. The rain was still pounding the windshield but the thunder and lightning had let up quite a bit.

I parked near the door and went into to grab a blanket for my freezing passenger. Beck was sound asleep on the couch so I gave her a gentle shake to wake her up. I grabbed the afghan from the back of the couch and went to retrieve Harley. Harley was completely out and I described everything to Rebecca and she and I managed Harley inside, and up to her bed, Rebecca tucked her in and reassured Prestly that her roommate was back. Beck and I readied for bed and we crashed, hard.

The morning cell phone alarms came bright and early and it took everything I had in me to drag my butt out of bed. Rebecca suggested that I take it easy and sleep in a bit, I reminded her that she had to work anyways and the horses would be kicking at the stalls demanding to be fed if I ignored them too long. I got out of bed and dressed as Beck woke most of the other girls. Beck left the cordless phone with Harley and a sticky note with our cell phone numbers on it.

The three girls and I tirelessly fumbled through our chores, we each dragged butt pretty bad. Rebecca made a warm breakfast for us before heading out to work. Madeline was concerned about Harley and asked all sorts of questions. Prestly and Jordan sped through their chores and took on the extra work now that Harley was unable to carry her weight. I lead the girls back in to get fed and ready for the school bus. We ate quickly and I was already tired and planning my nap. Banjo was harassing the girls as they readied for school, Prestly got dressed and what not in the bathroom and tiptoed around her room to avoid waking Harley.

After the girls loaded the bus, I took my position on the couch with Banjo for an early morning nap. Banjo leaped off of me waking me up after two hours of sleeping, I took it as Harley was up and about, I rolled off the couch and to my feet to head upstairs to check on her . I knocked on her door and asked if she needed any help. She yelled out that she did and to wait a second before letting myself in. Harley couldn't get her sweatpants on over her cast and kept herself covered so I could get her sweats up to her knees and let her do the rest. Harley gathered her

crutches and followed me down the stairs, she was
wobbly at first but got around fairly well.

Harley hurt and took her morning meds to
stave off the leg pain. I spoke to Harley that I had
a few chores to deal with and I suggested she
camp out with Banjo on the couch and take it easy.
Harley didn't fight the idea and quickly made it
happen. I fixed all of the clocks back to the right
times and then headed out to load up some
chickens and eggs for Sampsons. Banjo stayed
behind with Harley as I went to the market. I
greeted Sampson and told him about the nights'
adventure, he felt sorry for Harley and offered a
hand if there was anything he could do. He was
impressed that each of the girls took charge and
excelled.

We chatted for a bit at how well the girls
had taken charge and courageously headed into the
unknown and without hesitation, and how each took
on the role of rescuer.

I went back to the farm to check in on my guest and make sure that she was staying comfortable. When I got home things seemed awry. I couldn't find Harley on the couch where I left her and she didn't respond to my shouting when I called for her. I headed upstairs to try to find her and located her in the bathroom. She shouted through the door that Banjo was perched at, that she was fine and bathing crudely with a washcloth to get more of the mud off of her. I went back downstairs and put away the groceries from the market. I was glad that she was OK and Banjo came to join me as Harley was crutching down the stairs.

Harley sat at the table and let me wait on her. She wanted to share her newest trick with Banjo, she waved her upright right pinkey and said "phone" to him, and off he ran to fetch the cordless phone for her. Apparently she had a mildly productive morning increasing his skills to better help her while she was laid up. Harley and I spoke about her return to school the next day and I shot Mike a text about her situation so he was up to speed. The next phone call was to her mother Jill. I felt sort of bad that Harleys parents weren't filled in as soon as things happened but it was late.

Jill answered her work phone, I had a large lump in my throat as I greeted her. I calmly opened by explaining that Harley was OK and everything was going to be fine, Jill wasn't happy to hear that her daughter had been hurt but trusted her to be an adult and get through it with her tough attitude. Jill wasn't mad about everything and told me that she would tell Paul herself. Harley and Jill spoke and caught up about the whole hospital visit. Harley was a bit shaken having to go to the hospital, her last time didn't end up so well so I understood her stance.

I chatted with Harley as we both lazed out on the couches and watched different shows. Harley spoke about her last hospital visit that left her without the use of her two left fingers, she spoke about how much she hated being temporarily crippled or permanently scarred on her arm. Harley really opened up and described her anger towards her once best friend, Aiden, turning her back on her. I tried to console her as best as I could and just listened the rest of the time.

I told Harley that she could be the only one to forgive herself in her whole ordeal and that only she had the power to do that. I could tell by her biting her lip that she had something on her mind. Harley asked if I would mind her getting online and if she could just poke around for a bit. I reminded her that MyFace wasn't allowed and that other social media wasn't permitted either, she acknowledged that she understood and wanted to just browse to change things up. I headed out to turn over the manure pile, Banjo stayed behind to keep Harley company and I got to work in the nicer weather.

I turned over the smelly pile of manure and stopped often to survey the farm pastures. I took a break to walk over to Lemmy and see if maybe now we had become friends. Lemmy actually came towards me when I called him, I was surprised and greeted the much more gentle creature. I petted Lemmy for a bit and thanked him again for becoming much more reliable. I finished my chores and checked on Harley, she was set up at the computer with a pen and notebook handy and just responded without breaking her concentration. I let her know that the rest of the girls would be home soon and to call me if she needed anything then went back outside.

I grabbed a saddle and blanket and saddled up Lemmy. I lead him into the empty sheep pasture and climbed up onto him. I had a sense that Lemmy wanted to run in a much more open pen and I gave him a heel kick in approval. Lemmy started out with a mild run but as I leaned closer to his mane flowing in my face, I yelled to him that he could go ahead and go all out. Lemmy took the command and began to run all out, his stride was long and I could tell he loved it, this was it, this was what he had been waiting for, a hard run and unheeded openness. Lemmy and I circled the pasture several times and I kept a tight grip on his reigns and just let him run all he wanted. After a solid half hour of running and then slowing down, I patted Lemmy on the shoulders and encouraged him that he was a good boy, I was really impressed that he let himself be free and I promised him I would run him more often.

I dismounted Lemmy to open the gate, he didn't even try to yank his reigns out of my hands or try to kick me. Lemmy had a whole new attitude about him and he even let me keep petting him on his snout without jerking his head back in his usual "screw you buddy attitude." I walked Lemmy back to his paddock as the girls got off the bus. I carried the saddle back to the tack room in the barn and headed to the house to greet the girls. Harley was back on the couch when I entered and I caught up with the ladies and how their day was. Each girl had fared well and was glad their day was over with. Harley was updated on the homework and informed them that she would be back to school the next day.

I was curious to what Harley had been so motivated to work on online but waited for the room to clear before asking her about her business. Harley let me know she was just poking around some info and that it was "all good" I reminded her about the honesty policy at the ranch and she just responded that it was OK and that she'd let know when the time was right. I took votes about dinner ideas and Prestly and Madeline took their turn to cook. Jordan went out for her run with Banjo and I kicked it with Harley watching some of the Psych episodes I had stored on TV. The house began to smell pretty good and the girls were mum on what they were up to so I just trusted all of the young adults around me and tried to keep my mind from wandering.

We feasted on jumbalaya and to the credit of the cooks, it was superb. Beck came home from dinner and caught up with each of the girls. The rest of the week went smoothly getting Harley used to crutching to and fro between classes and on and off the bus. Harley healed and May came to an end. I kept up with many cook outs and it was always nice to have guests over. At the end of May I was due for a hay cutting and I still had 3 girls able to help out. We all rode the wagon and stacked the hay bales that spat out of the baler. We got sweaty and dirty as we worked on the weekend and the girls did very well.

After all of the work was done, we lounged about on the patio and let the night wind down.

Harley was now in a brace as her leg was only a few weeks away from being free from entrapment. Harley kept spending time online and Jordan was getting busier with her business ordering and stocking of inventory. She was mere weeks away from opening and Corina moved their apartment to one that was atop of the business. The business had three apartments above it and Corina was able to find renters for the other two to help make more money towards the rent to ease the financial burdens of the business until it was fully independent.

Prestly and Madeline enjoyed working with the horses, Prestly was more than ready to get back to New Mexico and no one could blame the ones that wanted to get back home. Neither Beck or I took any offense when they spoke about going back home because we knew this point would arrive. I sensed Madeline was still hesitant about going home, her attacker was a family member and that was a situation she would never be able to escape.

After the guests had gone, Beck and I spoke about the girls. We were very proud of how far they had come since they had first arrived, timid and scared. Harley had become rather humbled having to crutch around life for the month and the chip she carried so adamantly with her has now gone. Harley was much more beautiful now that she wasn't angry at the world. Each girl flourished in their own way and Beck was so glad her dream had worked out so well. Beck was contemplating searching again for another group of girls to replace our initial group, to see if there were more that we could help and to keep our farm teeming with life. The most beautiful thing a girl can wear is confidence, when a lady holds herself higher than she feels, everyone should tip their hat.

I spent a school day getting everything situated for the flights home. I arranged with the parents for pickups for when the girls got to their home airports and things were coming to an end. Beck and I joined Felicia for a group session and suggested that each girl embrace their parents and tell them about their histories. Once again Jordan skirted the need to do so as her future had taken a rather significant turn to the positive. The other three girls had become antsy at the thought of telling their parents about the rapes, molestings, or their getting cornered in life. Madeline started to cry at the thought of having to face her parents and tell them that the cousin they left in charge, fondled her at such a young age.

Harley said she was ready to tell Jill and Paul about Sebastian and his friend Shawn taking turns raping her one night after the school dance. Harley wanted to kick the crap out of Aiden for all of her parts involved with her school life going into the toilet. Harley was ready to be free of her brace and get back to kickboxing and into great physical shape, and also to embrace her mock military school cover she took on while she was away for the school year. Prestly was worried

about what might happen at school when she came
forward about the upper classman and his strange
stalking that he did, not to mention sexually
abusing her in the park that night.

Beck was proud of each of them and let
them know that we could be there for them if any
of them needed us to be, for anything. Two weeks
to go before the out flux of bodies were to happen,
flights were arranged and the girls had begun
packing things up preemptively and anxiously ready
to head home. I was going to miss the girls and
Beck was semi emotional when we spoke about them
all flying out in mid-June. Randy stopped by in early
June for a night of wrenching on buckshot and
Harley sat by and just watched. Randy and I spoke
about rebuilding the engine and I was thinking
about taking Winston up on his offer to beef up
the V-8. Harley asked a few questions here and
there about some of the trucks components.

Rebecca stayed in the house with the other
girls and they giggled away the evening in a girly
gathering. Harley wasn't one for the girly nights
anyways so she didn't mind passing up on them. I
was not thrilled to be exposed to the gaggle of
laughing and carrying on. The night carried on and
even as it grew dark out, the oldies played on in the
garage as Randy and I toiled away on buckshot.
Harley retired for the night and hobbled back
inside, she was supposed to keep on her crutches
but she was rebellious and carried them with her
most of the time by now.

The conversation among the girls centered around their going home more and more as each day brought the morning farm chores, and after school as well. Beck and I supported each lady and expressed our gratitude for their help and also at our respect for the steps they had each taken to improve their lives, and ours. The girls cooked more and more each night and we spent ample time hanging out in our groups just shooting the breeze. Jordan kept up on her running and once Harley was free from her fabric brace, she was back to hitting the punching bag once again.

Prestly was sad to leave behind the horses she had grown fond of, Harpo had continued her funny whispering in the ears of unsuspecting victims, occasionally getting girls to jump early in the mornings. I still wished harder that Madeline had more confidence in herself to face her struggles that lay before her, I hoped that she would be able to take them on with grace and poise.

Beck and I stayed up most nights after the girls had gone to bed and discussed what might be in store for each of them, Rebecca really hoped that they each keep in contact as she had really gotten close with them. I also hoped to continue to hear from the ladies after they went home but I deeply felt that we might have just been a layover stop in their life. We offered each of them a place to find solace, a chance to gain inner peace and hoped that they each found the courage to blossom into full adults. Beck and I each joked about how great it would be to get Christmas cards or random emails from them to remain included in their lives.

I was pretty sure that Beck would keep up with the girls' lives through their mothers, they all had much closer relationships and girls usually worked like that anyways. I left more of the social intricacies to my wife with the exceptions of the guys I interacted with, Mike, Sampson, and Randy. Things were winding both up and down as the first week of June came to a close. The girls were getting more excited about going home, getting ready for the ending of another school year. Beck and I were trying to keep our game faces and trying to remain strong and not show our sadness to see them go.

The girls were all signed up to fly out the Sunday after school subsided. I had a large grilling party planned for the girls as a send off cookout. Winston was headed out to Florida U. in August as he had transferred his credits and passed the tests necessary to become a student. Mike and Annie hugged the girls and thanked them for being apt students and doing so very well in their classes. Felicia was emotional about their departure and expressed how glad she was to be able to get to know them each individually and also as a group. The girls were their happy giggling selves but also sad that they were going to be departing from the friendships that they had built among them here.

The girls were so thankful for everything that we had done and the insight into adulthood that we had shared. They also thanked and hugged us for housing them and offering to open our lives to them. Beck and I each shared last words of wisdom that we could muster and suggested that they each follow their hearts, we knew that leaving their lives behind and coming to Michigan all by themselves must have been scary. It really must have taken courage to come live with strangers, even if the courage was masked by desperation, it was still there.

The girls took some of the horses out for one last group ride, Beck and Felicia joined them as they snaked through the woods, Beck rode Lemmy and he took to being ridden by her very well. I sat back with Sampson and the two brothers and spoke about what else was looming in the upcoming summer. Sampson spoke about hiring a new butcher as his market required a lot of his time already and Mike was looking to take a cruise with his wife during their summer break, some Alaskan sightseeing something ar another. Things were winding down and tapering off to an ending for this whole ordeal.

The final Sunday seemed to have arrived too soon. All of the girls loaded their things into the bed of my truck and everyone loaded in accordingly. Banjo sat in the back with Prestly, Madeline and Harley as Jordan rode shotgun and Rebecca in the middle. The girls all voted that Banjo had to go and needed to ride in the cab with them so they could all get plenty of goodbye pats in. Beck was misty eyed as we headed to Detroit Metro to send the girls off one at a time. We arrived with plenty of time to get each young lady checked in and make sure all of the flight stuff was on time and that they were ready to go.

Jordan was the first to depart, I loaded all of her belongings onto the conveyor belt and we all said our goodbyes. Each of the girls cried and gave big hugs. The girls had all exchanged contact information so they could stay in touch over the summer, Harley and Prestly both suggested that they try and all get together once in a while in each others' hometowns. Beck and I both offered that they were all welcome at anytime for any reason if they wanted to come visit. Madeline remained fairly quiet but was charitable with hugs. The girls had become very close and it was a very nice sight to see them all hugging and bidding each other safe flights. It was a long school year and so many things had changed since the beginning, it was all surreal sitting here and watching my temporary daughters leave for good.

Prestly was next up for departing, she was headed straight to New Mexico and she was the most ready to get back home, out of all of our guests. Prestly hugged Beck and I and couldn't express her appreciation enough for words but her tight hug and dripping eyes said more than she needed to. I was so proud of each of these girls and even though they each brought more baggage to the farm than their luggage, they seemed to have broadened and grown well past the frightened, troubled young girls they were when they arrived.

The girls all said their goodbyes and Prestly sauntered into the airport, this was it, our final farewells to the young girl. Harley and Madeline wept in the back seat as they were the only two remaining girls left. Harley's flight was half an hour out and she was mixed with many emotions. Harley was rigid and closed off when she arrived, refused to open up and hell bent on making it on her own. Harley was still the toughest girl I had ever met but her transition into a tender and loving young lady was a wonderful improvement. Harley had impressed me the most with her ability to acclimate to her surroundings and still take charge, even with her breaking her leg.

Harley was more than willing to step up and saddle up to help round up stray cows. Harley never showed any fear, I suspected her anger towards the hospital stay was fear based, she still fought her urge to resist and charged into it no matter the consequences. I told Harley that it was her time and that no matter what, don't go back to being closed off. People risk hurting you but that hurt can only happen because you took the chance to trust. Much like she initially trusted Aiden to be her friend, she has since trusted each of us on the farm with her inner demons and after doing so, she learned that there were still safe people in the world to trust.

Harley was crying quite hard as she gathered her carry on and recited her flight number to North Carolina. Harley hugged Rebecca tightly and myself even more tightly. She then hugged Madeline and told Madeline that she needn't be a stranger. With a last pet to Banjo, Harley turned and strolled into the airport. Beck and I were extremely sad to watch Harley go, she was rough when she arrived but with time and the yearning to trust, she made the most progress of all of the girls and she had the pride of both of us.

Madeline sniffled and dried her eyes and then it was just us.

Madelines flight was a bit of time away, Beck and I were getting hungry and we held off the conversation of food until after our last guest had left us. We spoke about the night of the storm, Banjo and his goofy antics like his muddy belly crawl across the kitchen floor and things he had done. Madeline was being social and kept repeating thanks to us. We tried to leave her with lasting words of courage. I strongly suggested that she let herself laugh, flip through all of her sketches of the horses and pictures of the lambs that she drew. Beck suggested that she seek further help to get her over her severe mental obstacle: Charlie.

Madeline nodded as we spoke but it seemed to fall on deaf ears. Madeline was still very thin and a gorgeous blonde girl and could do so many things with her life if she could get past her childhood trauma and let life be her easle. Madeline was very talented, she handed over a drawing she made of Rebecca and I sitting on our patio bench, the pencil shading was absolutely amazing, I told Beck that the first thing to happen when we got home was to frame it for the living room. Time drew near for her flight and she got ever more nervous to board. Beck and Madeline hugged for a long time and I just pet Banjo to keep him calm.

Madeline and Beck broke their embrace and she then turned her teary self towards me. I hugged the petite girl and told her that she was stronger than she could ever imagine if she just tried. I recommended to the young girl that she confide in people and give them a chance to be trustworthy. Beck made sure that she had our numbers and knew of our routines, and also reassured her that we would always be available to speak to if she ever needed to just talk. Madeline wiped her eyes but just as quickly, they watered back up again.

Madeline turned to the airport entrance and started her way in. She turned momentarily and looked back to thank us again. I held my wife close, it felt like we had sent our own children off and might never see them again. It was just Rebecca and I now, Banjo laid in the backseat and just kinda whimpered. I could tell that Banjo knew what was going on and he seemed sad about his friends that were gone.

Beck put the front middle seat down and strapped on her seat belt. We jostled back and forth different ideas for dinner and whatever we decided, we'd let Banjo out for a bathroom break and knew he'd sit in the truck and behave. I shifted into drive and we made out way back to I94 and headed home. We stopped off at a local restaurant and ate quietly as we contemplated what might lie instore for our young girls. We were both in a bitter sweet mood, glad that we had the chance to make a hopefully positive impression on the girls but also sad to see them go.

We made it back to the farm as the first text came through, Harley made it home first, shortly after Jordan then Prestly. Madelines' flight landed another half hour after the prior girls'. That was it, the girls were home and our trial school year was over. I laid awake next to my wife that night, things seemed extra quiet with a now empty house. I was thinking I would be relieved to have the house back with my wife and I but I missed knowing that the girls were sleeping down the hallway, safely, it was weird.

Neither Beck or I slept well that night, we got to our chores and things settled back into the routine that we construed before the arrival of four lost girls in the prior fall. We rehashed several stories of the girls and Harpo making them each jump with her playful whispering. We sadly missed the girls as we worked around the farm. Over the next few weeks, we received some emails about the home transitions of the girls, each made it home just fine and settled back into their lives that had been changed when they came to us at the ranch.

Harley called me one night and expressed that she needed to come clean. Harley had been researching laws so she had all of the necessary information to persue criminal charges against her attackers and had contacted a lawyer to do it.

Harley had pressed formal charges against the two men that ravaged her so brutally and her case looked pretty solid. Harley apologized about being secretive but felt she had to do it alone because that it how things would be back home. Paul and Jill supported their daughter and offered any help that she might need, she just wanted to apologize for not being very forthcoming. Beck and I reassured her that everything was OK and that we hoped things went well for her.

Jordan had opened her store for the first time the day after she got back to Arizona, her quick internet marketing had gotten her pretty good foot traffic with the running crowds in the area and things looked good for her as a business owner. I was inspired by Jordans hard work and was very happy to hear that her sales were increasing over the summer and that things looked up in a big way for her. Things were mildly quiet from Prestly and Madeline but Beck got emails from the parents for updates. Both girls had gotten back to their lives as June closed out, everything seemed to get back to the normal for everyone involved, things were at peace.

Fourth of July weekend was upon Beck and I at the Farm. I was ramping up for a big barbecue for the friends and it was looking like it was going to be a good one. Beck made her green apple sangria and I braised a rack of lamb for the grill. I wondered how the girls were all doing in their lives and I had only half the places to set for dinner. Banjo was still growling at the damn chickens and I couldn't drag him away fast enough. Mike and Annie showed up with Randy close behind. Sampson was going to run a little later as he was working later keeping his market open for his patrons on the holiday.

The horses were all in their paddocks and the sheep grazing about. All of us adults were eating and drinking our fill. We spoke about the farm and individual lives and mentioned the girls once in a while in our conversations. The night carried on, as we all did and it was a good time. We all enjoyed the company of one another and took a great calming relief in the ambient environment of the farm, the tranquility is everything anyone would need to cure anything life may load on someone. Beck and I climbed into bed after all was said and done, Banjo kept to his grilled bone in the kitchen and that was that for the night.

Monday came and Beck had to work, I was solo for the chores and it still seemed to take me longer than it had when I had plenty of help from the school year guests. I missed the crazy mornings with all of the girls struggling to get dressed and out to the barn work. The barns were so much more calm without all of the extra bodies, the horses even seemed more somber than usual. I partook to being the role model and what not and now I could carry myself a little loser and breath easier without having to keep an eagle eye on a bunch of almost adults rummaging about among the stalls.

I finished my morning routine and headed inside to finish my Irish tea and change out for the rest of my day. Banjo was close behind me until I went inside, I suspected that he headed over to the chicken pen to be a pest or roll around in the garden to give me something else to do that day. I sat at the table and just eased through the rest of my dark brewed tea. Suddenly the phone rang, I was curious who would be calling my house phone as

Sampson and Beck always called my cell. Erin Armstrong was on the other end of the phone.

I was surprised to hear from Erin, usually she dealt with Rebecca when it came to the girls. I tried to greet her but quickly stopped as I could hear her trying not to cry through the phone she was upset. My stomach sank immediately and dread took over me, my heart pounded in my ears. I couldn't stop my head from spinning and I laid it on my forearm to keep from falling off of my chair, my eyes went blurry as tears began to well up. Mrs. Armstrong told me that Madeline had killed herself the previous night. Erin had to force herself to blurt out the news before she went back to crying uncontrollably, I was overwhelmed.

My stomach started to do back flips in my gut, I tried to swallow really hard to ask her what happened. Erin just kept weeping when suddenly Ricks stern voice picked up the phone. Rick told me that they had a large family gathering for the firework filled holiday and Madeline was in course shape with everyone there. Madeline had avoided most of the family and when Erin had confronted Madeline about why she was so standoffish, ever more than usual. Madeline opened up to Erin and spilled all of her demons to her. Erin called the police while Charlie was still there and had him arrested, the situation with Charlie caused a huge scene and things went crazy.

The family was quickly divided and half of them started blaming Madeline. Erin found it absolutely absurd that anyone would think any of the horrors were Madeline's fault, how could the victim be the reason some out of control pervert did what he did? It was asinine, and it caused all of the family to take sides as Charlie was loaded into a squad car. After the family was gone and angers extinguished momentarily, the Armstrongs retired home for the evening. Madeline didn't want to talk to anyone and went to her room. The family had so much tearing at the seams that held them together and Erin and Rick needed so many more answers than were available and they expected Madeline to speak up and relive everything all over again.

Erin told Rick everything while they were alone for the short while. Rick wanted to kill Charlie and he pieced everything together and it explained so much about why she was such a silent withdrawn little girl. Rick went up to talk to Madeline and there was no response when he knocked on the door. Rick had to shoulder through the door and that's when he found her. Madeline had sent a few emails out to the other girls and one to Rebecca. Madeline also sent a deeply apologetic letter to her parents, describing everything that had happened and that she couldn't live this way anymore, being the cause of all the new family animosity was too much for her anymore, Madeline couldn't live with such a burden any longer.

Madeline wrote down everything she had purged herself of at the farm during the intense tell all and hoped that it was enough to get Charlie sentenced appropriately for what he had done but she wasn't strong enough to heal and move forward with her life. I felt just sick and I started to cry with my whole body as Rick told me about the upcoming funeral plans. I assured Mr. Armstrong that my wife and I would be there. I used the house phone to call Rebecca at work and texted Randy that I had an emergency need for him to watch the farm for the next few days.

I contacted Rebecca, she hadn't checked her email yet as she usually did at the end of her work days while finishing reports of her day. I told Rebecca to sit down, she could tell immediately from the tone of my voice that it was no good. I told her that Erin had called me and what had happened. Beck was distraught with grief. My wife cried and I couldn't make out anything that she was saying so I told her I was coming to get her.

I packed up Banjo and raced to pick Rebecca up. I sped to the hospital and texted Felicia the update, I know better than to text and drive but this situation was emergent enough to warrant breaking the law for a bit. I headed up to Becks floor and asked my way around to find her. I was still tearing up and full of disbelief as I found her. Beck stood up and let me hold her tightly when I entered her office. I felt like I was at such a loss and didn't know what to do. My phone dinged with a response from Felicia and I coaxed Rebecca down and out to the truck where Banjo was waiting for us. Beck and I tried to speak but were mostly inaudible in a murmuring slurring blubbering way between deep sniffle filled sobs among us while Banjo just sat his head on my wifes lap trying to comfort her.

I headed back to the farm so we could pack and get flights arranged for a speedy departure. We couldn't get seats side by side but we got seats booked on the same flight. Randy came barreling through the gates as we were loading up to leave. I gave Randy the quick update as we loaded up to head out. Rebecca called each of the girls and gave them the news as we drove to the airport. I texted Randy my credit card info and the girls phone numbers and asked him to get all of them to Indiana as soon as possible. We parked the truck in the long term parking and hustled our way into the airport.

I texted Randy thanks and we loaded onto the flight. We landed in Indiana again and I sent Rebecca for the luggage as I scored us a rental before going back to get her at the luggage carousel. We started the hour drive to Madelines' hometown and Beck used her phone to call and make hotel reservations. I got a text from Randy that informed me that the girls were already on their way and would all be at the airport within a few hours. I dropped Rebecca off at the hotel to relax for a bit and turned back to get the girls.

My head still spun with all of the news about young Madeline. I had so many questions that would remain unanswered and I would have to figure it out in time. Jordan and Harley were waiting together to get picked up and let me know that Prestly was only a few minutes behind. Jordan sprung for all of the flights as her business had been doing extremely well for her, I was impressed as how well they organized and how quickly to make it from their respective parts of the country to get here for their friend and roommate.

Jordan was on a flight half an hour after Rebecca called her and she would figure out the rest from there. Prestly was half an hour behind the girls in landing but then there were all three of them packed into my car as we headed through Indiana. The girls each cried and hugged for the entire drive. I sent the girls to my room as I booked another room for them to share when we were back in the hotel. Rebecca was still an emotional wreck when I met up with all four of them in my room. Each of the girls helped grab all of the gear and moved to their room across the hall. I gave them a half hour time limit to get ready and we would head to the Armstrong's house swiftly.

We loaded up as the sky began to set, it was a grim mood in the car, sided with an adequate amount of crying. I fought my best to remain held together but it wasn't easy. I thought I was sad finding out that Beck and I weren't able to have kids but I suddenly lost a daughter and I had no idea how to handle it. The girls all spoke about their flights and the month of homelife they each had before this impromptu meeting. The girls tried to joke a bit between tears, mention of Banjo came up among the conversations within the car as we made our way south. We followed the same path Beck and I had taken almost a year ago when we first met up with the Armstrongs for dinner. We followed the GPS directions to the house and it wasn't far from the diner we ate at back then.

We arrived to the Victorian bungalow and knocked at the door, it was full of people but Rick answered the door. Rick was in a suit and you could tell he was upset and very emotional, his hand shook as he reached out to shake my hand. Beck gave him a hug and proceeded to introduce the girls that had joined us. Rick was surprised that we managed to round up and all join them for Madeline on such short notice. We made our way through the house to find Erin sitting on the couch sobbing still.

The funeral was the next two days but that first night was an informal family gathering. People looked hungry, I knew what we could do and got to it. I took a body count of the twenty or so people that were in the house and nodded to Harley to come with me. I recommended that Prestly and Jordan play host as best they could and to keep eyes on Beck and Erin. Harley and I headed out to find a grocery store and we promptly filled a shopping cart with enough to feed the army back at the house. I knew that even though upset, the girls would step up to take care of the family of the friend they just lost. Much like the night of the storm, I knew that despite the strong emotional upset, that these girls had the inner strength to do what was right, the inner strength they didn't have a year ago.

Harley and I carried groceries back into the house where the other girls had already made them selves acquainted with the kitchen. I played head chef with the girls as we made the always quick and easy pasta with white sauce for everyone. Neither Rebecca or Erin ate much but measly picked at some of the salad bits just to give themselves something to do. Most of the other random family members ate and all were gracious for the home cooked meal rather than ordering out. The girls took charge and cleaned up after everyone, they really stepped up in a big way. I tried to remain focused on the mood of the occasion but I still took pride in how the girls had blossomed in their personalities as well as their moral character.

Jordan had lost some weight over the few weeks since we had seen her, she had started eating much cleaner and followed many of the better eating habits she had found within her running magazines she sold on her store racks.

Harley had followed Becks lead and added
highlights to her hair and Prestly had cut hers a
bit. The girls were all looking happy and well after
three weeks back in their lives. Each girl had shed
many of the worries they initially ran from when
they came to the ranch, maybe each girl just
needed the off school year to establish who they
were, or maybe the time to practice living as who
they wanted to become, safe, confident, and
reinforced to be an adult. The girls each had taken
charge in their own lives and realized how petty
others' can be when it comes to how they were
treated.

We loaded up after the solemn evening and headed back to the hotel for some rest before the long two days that were ahead of us. I bid the girls goodnight and tucked my exhausted wife into bed. From the noise in the hallway it sounded like the girls were going to make use of the swimming facilities on the lower floor, part of me wanted to go and keep an eye on them but I just trusted the young adults to act accordingly. I laid in bed just reflecting on all of the turmoil that festered in my brain, I just couldn't grasp how Madeline could have gone through with what she did, she knew she was welcome back with us anytime and if she needed more time than she could have gotten it. Utterly I could only fathom that she looked down the road to her future and came to the realization that her only future memories only held fear and remorse for what had happened and maybe she felt she could never be free of her past.

The next morning came after a night of restless sleep. Beck and I readied and called the girls' room to let them know when we were heading out. We all gathered up around ten-thirty and stopped off for a late breakfast before going to stand post in the funeral home. The girls chatted in the back seat but mostly in hush tones mixed with crying. The girls tried to up the mood while we ate, they spoke about playing around in the pool and laughing so hard, "tears ran down their thighs", I found comedy in the expression. I was glad to have the girls back in our company and despite the grim circumstances, it was still pretty nice.

We loaded back up and headed to the funeral parlor. Prestly had never seen a deceased person before and she was extra nervous that it would be the last time Madeline would be seen by any of us. I took a deep breath making the same realization. We all fought to keep from being overtaken with grief but even with fake smiles or forced positive topics of conversation, it always reverted back to poor little Madeline and the weeping was always starting all over again.

The parlor was monotone and calm on the outside as we parked and made our way in. We each took a deep breath and let out large sighs one at a time before stepping inside. Each of the girls were dressed respectfully and we all did our best to put on our strong faces before heading into the viewing room. The girls were each arm in arm and I reminded them to stay together and be strong. I had warned the girls that this wasn't going to be easy and that they should hold each other close. Beck held my hand so tight I could feel my fingers turning blue. I could feel my eyes well up again and I contemplated purposefully dehydrating myself to the point of no longer producing tears so I could remain the strong one of the group.

The room was cold and full of people dressed for the occasion. We made our rounds between all of the pictures of Madeline and family members, each introducing one another. It was pleasant to see so many people that loved Madeline and we each wished she had felt the love that filled the room. Madeline was layed out quietly and looked to be finally at peace. Rebecca lost it seeing her adopted daughter in her casket and it felt like a punch in the gut when I finally had to courage to pay my respects. Each of the girls expressed their pains and sorrows in accordance with their personalities. I could see Harley clenching her jaw to fight her emotions while Jordan tried to focus on anything else in the room. Prestly had to almost be dragged to the casket side by the other two in order to actually make her viewing happen.

The first day was very long and drawn out, we took a bit of a break to catch a bite of food and brought back things for Rick and Erin to eat as they refused to leave even for a minute. Neither parent wanted to lose any last moment to spend with their daughter before she was promised to the ground. I tried to be the caretaker of all I had brought as well as the Armstrongs. Beck remained in proximity with Erin as Rick tried his best to man-up and make pleasantries with everyone visiting the funeral home. The girls predominately hung near a large poster covered with a photo timeline of the young girls' life.

Rick and Erin were very gracious for all of the help as well as the quick trip to Indiana from all of us. Erin told the girls about all of the stories that she had heard from the ranch, she squeaked out a few smiles behind tears as she imagined Madeline befriending each girl and sharing adventures with them. She was glad to see that Harley was OK after her fall and was thrilled to hear Jordan was being successful in her ambitious decision. After the first day at the funeral home we were all ready to get to the hotel and attempt to unwind a bit. I convinced Rebecca to join me in the hot tub to relax.

The girls joined us in the hot tub and had some interesting news to share. Harley piped up and told us that she had pressed charges against her attackers, she had loaded her lawyer up with case info that she had uncovered while online back at the farm. Beck and I were amazed as the willingness to really put herself out there for the sake of justice. Prestly joined her in her legal action pursuit as she had sought criminal actions against the guy that assaulted her at the park and blackmailed her in school.

Beck and I were so profoundly happy to hear the new found strength within the girls themselves and each one had a valiant sense of confidence. We stayed late boiling like lobsters in the hot tub before getting back to bed. We caught up more with the girls and their newer future plans, it was nice to hear that they were each looking at their futures with more endeavors than they had considered before this past school year. The last day was cut short with the burial. The procession was long and contained more cars that the town itself had in it. There were so many sad faces standing in that cemetery sun on that Wednesday afternoon in July.

We loaded up our things after the final flowers were laid on Madelines' final resting place and we each said our goodbyes to the Armstrongs. We kinda milled around and struggled to make peace with everything that had happened, we knew we would never get to speak with Madeline again or see her either. The memories we had with her were all we would ever have again. As I've said, life is just memories strung together, we had some pretty good memories that included Madeline but Rebecca and I had hoped that maybe these girls would make spontaneous visits to us up in Michigan as life progressed. We had hoped for wedding invitations or family pictures as these ladies had built families and maybe we would become foster grandparents and always be in their lives.

We each finally agreed it was time to saddle up and ride into the horizon. As the gathering at the cemetery dwindled and people departed from the mix, we spoke about the idea of maybe coming back to pay our respects once a year. With college and what-not coming up for the girls, I suspected keeping to the agreement might be a challenge for the girls. We headed out to the airport to part one last time. We all took stock of how delicate life was and how much we would miss what we once had. Beck had a hard time for a while after losing the girls all over again and an even harder time with everything with Madeline.

Beck cared for each of the girls as if they were each our own, the loss reawakened all of her emotions regarding Kaylee but having to handle such a tragic situation all over again; she was better equipped. The rest of July was an emotional one and we sought comfort in our friends and with each other. Beck and I kept to our four-legged child and worked to keep the farm flourishing.

There are many nights we sit around and miss our girls, Madeline will always be missed the most. Life has many twists and turns, many obstacles that need to be overcome, the biggest obstacle someone can have, is themself. Rebecca and I know that as life goes on we'll acquire more and more memories and look down the road that is the future of life, we look forward to reliving so many memories that we've shared and held closely to one another while getting through. I loved my wife and I know that no matter what; she would be by my side and in retrospect, she knows that no matter what; I'll be by her side to make many more memories with.